BROKE DOWN
HOUSE

Broke Down House
Copyright © 2025
by C S Hughes
New Edition
Published by
Otherly Press ISBN
978-0-6459204-5-1
Contact
editor@otherly.press
All Rights Reserved

otherly press

Contents

"May we play outside, Father?" Alwyn looked at Robert, his brother, his twin, exactly alike. Same hair, same clothes, same conspiratorial smile. The only difference was, one held the toy aeroplane with its wide wings and red propeller. Which one? They'd never tell.

"Of course, Robert, but only for a little while, and don't play in the woods."

Father's face crumpled, suddenly. Like Christmas paper. Alwyn didn't know why.

"Yes, Father!" The boys shouted in chorus. They ran through the lounge for the front door, kicking aside discarded wrappings like leaves, past the kitchen where Mother in her Christmas apron, opening oven doors and stirring pots with practiced efficiency, nevertheless had time to turn with a smile and a wave as they passed, the aroma of roasting turkey so enticing, it guaranteed they would come when called.

"Mmmmm, yum," the boys said in unison, passing.

"I seem to have cooked too much," Mother said, brow creasing. There was a smear of red like a tear on the otherwise neat expanse of her green and white apron. Cranberry sauce, Robert thought. "Don't go too far."

"We'll just be playing aeroplanes," Alwyn said, as Robert flew by, arms outstretched and zooming.

Outside it was a crisp, still morning. Bells echoed from the village church, beyond the stand of bare-limbed trees that edged the yard. Robert stood in the shadow of the wood, winding the propeller, tightening the elastic band. Alwyn waited by the house, on the sere winter lawn between the path and the woodpile, flexing fingers inside woollen gloves.

Robert launched it with an awkward throw, trying for maximum height. The plane bit the air with an insect whirr, diving upwards in starts, curving in a glide to the other side of the woodpile.

"A little off course, but good!" Alwyn shouted. He ran over, retrieving the plane, noticing for a moment the shapes inside. Mother stopped placing settings at the table, father hugged her.

Alwyn turned, winding it for his go.

"Hey, these ailerons in the wings are adjustable!" He set them as evenly as he could, for a straight, steady flight. Instead of throwing, he let go, relying on the propellor to take it up. It flew in a long upward climb, then curved down, above Robert's reaching fingers, into the shadows under the trees.

"Spectacular!" Robert found it without too much trouble, in the leaves and snow under the bone-bare trees. He thought, I can get a better distance than that.

"I'm going to take her to the rise!" he shouted.

"No, you mustn't. Lunch is soon, Father said not to!" Alwyn walked up to the wood, and stood staring at his brother. Robert was always the bolder.

The rise was a cliff high in the woods, above a creek, looking out across the valley. Mountains grey in the distance.

"If you fly her from there, she'll be lost. How will we get her back?"

"Stop being a spoil sport! Come and see her fly!"

"You mustn't!" He was pacing up and down, fretting, as his brother moved deeper into the woods, He could barely see him now.

The back door banged. Father was there. "Alwyn, come in, it's lunch."

"I can't."

"Have you lost your plane?"

"Robert has taken it to the rise. He's going to fly it there. He's going to lose it."

"I'll help you look. Not a word to your mother, you know how upset she gets."

"But Robert took it!"

"You must stop this. I'll get you another. You know he fell, he died there a year ago."

"But look, he's almost gone!"

Thomas looked. In the shadows, amongst the drift and spindle trunks, perhaps something moved, something pale, looking back, something red and tinsel in its hand.

She seemed an ordinary woman, not overly given to hysteria, as she stood by the red phone fumbling in her purse for change with one hand, and with the other dragging the pram, stuffed with shopping bags, out of the way of shoppers proceeding down the mall.

This, however, required some dexterity, and was made considerably more difficult by the child, wearing a harness and straining at the end of the leather leash wrapped around her wrist. The toddler lurched forward, jerking her arm, so the pram teetered precariously. Unnoticed, a can of Campbell's Creamy Pumpkin soup fell out and rolled across the tiled floor as the pram dropped back onto all four wheels.

The toddler left wet nose and hand prints on the plate glass window of the butcher's shop, as his mother pulled him back from gazing at the display of meat within.

With the child momentarily under control she managed to deposit two coins in the phone slot, however, attracted again by the butcher's lurid arrangements, he began again straining at the leash.

"Come on Jimmy." She said exasperated, and jerked the leash so that he sat on the floor, and she pulled him sliding on his bottom back by the pram. However, as soon as she released the tension on the leash he scrabbled forward. She had finally to spank him so that he then clung to her leg weeping, his little hands twisting knots in the cotton of her skirt.

The youth was not necessarily bad, or drugged, or crazy, just at that stage of adolescence when rebellion against any constraint is a fulfilment of the spirit.

The toddler had dropped to his knees by his mother's feet as she spoke on the phone. The youth, woolly haired and a little wild, walking past, saw some humour in this tableaux.

He dropped to his hands and knees by the child, quite close to the woman's ankles, and started barking. The toddler caught on to the play immediately and began barking in return.

Curiously, the mother failed to notice for some few moments, until the youth began gambolling about quite exactly in the manner of a playful dog.

Suddenly horrified, she stood frozen, dropped the phone, her purse and let go the pram. The barking must have registered but she gave the youth only a cursory glance before crying out, "A dog is attacking my baby!"

She then began heaving on the leash so the child, delighted, began also jumping about like some puppet dog, yipping and yapping all the while.

The youth found this leaping about cause for further hilarity and barked and gambolled all the more.

A crowd gathered to watch this spectacle, uncertain as to its cause or meaning.

The mother now hoisted the child into the air, swinging him in an arc and crying, "Help! Help! A dog is attacking my baby!"

Some few in the crowd hearing the mother's cries also took up the refrain. A fat suited man, shouting, "Mad dog! Mad dog!" and nearly frothing at the mouth himself, swung a kick at the animal.

A constable then pushed past the onlookers. Hearing the cry of, "Mad dog!" He drew his revolver and shot the beast. Somehow caught in the frenzy of the crowd's delusion he also shot, with a boom that broke the illusion into a revealing silence, the woman's dog.

He was a skinny, handsome Indian man with a goofy smile and kind eyes.

"Now this shouldn't be a problem," he said. "I've helped people with all sorts of problems, smoking, weight loss, anxiety, depression, fear." He held her elbow as she lowered herself into the recliner, "I also do a stage show, it's very funny. I do this bit where I get a smoker from the audience, and I say, 'You are a chicken, you are a chicken, chickens don't smoke', and in an aside to the audience while the fellow is clucking and behaving like a chicken I say, 'What can I tell you, I also get the free eggs.' Oh that always get a laugh. Now relax."

After that she sank towards blackness, then a vortex. And she woke, chest heaving, standing above the doctor, on his knees, saying, "Something red, something red." There were three raised welts on his face. The receptionist was dragging her by the arm. The doctor was saying something in a language she didn't understand, and "Don't let her back."

Outside the sun hit her, harsh, blinding. Tears flooded from her eyes without reason. She didn't sob.

At home she fumbled with the keys, dashed into the bedroom but the insistent ringing of the phone ceased as she reached for it. Silence. The vibration of the phone, but not the noise, seemed to persist in the air. Her forehead was damp. She stepped out of biting shoes and lay on the bed.

She woke in darkness. There was a smell of damp earth, and the faintest cry, perhaps a stray cat. Or a baby crying in pain, need and exhaustion.

Seven thirty was a more reasonable time to awake, in the glare of a cloudless summer morning. She felt a twinge in her belly and skipped breakfast. A quick coffee and apple and pear juice in a box for the bus ride to work.

She'd forgot her sunglasses. Why was the sun so bright? She could see the heat in clouds of exhaust fumes billowing off the road.

She had a cat, it went away.

At church the preacher said how in olden times, "The way to God is over the ashes of the ungodly. And one of the marks of a witch were moles, which were known as 'The Devil's Teats. "

She shuddered to imagine Satan's little imps crawling stealthily over her skin and grasping the moles she had on her shoulder, chest, side, with sharp little claws, greedily suckling.

She remembered the feel of her mother's hands, soft but firm, holding her face.

"Who is she?" Mother would ask.

"She's the cat's mother." She'd reply.

Then the slap. Stinging, eyes watering. Her mother wore fake nails back then, long, crimson like talons. She still had pale traceries of scars on her cheek. She laughed then, a short gulp, at the thought of her mother's nails still growing, underground. How thick and crimson were they now? A spectre, sunken mouthed, hollow eyed, with lank long grey hair, rose up in her mind. Something red behind it. She shuddered, shook. The memory merged with the spectre. She felt the slap again. Rank, cold.

"Remember what I told you."

She'd hide in the bathroom.

She hid in the bathroom.

Clotted blood came out her nose in clumps, like drowned spiders, legs twitching, distending as they hit the damp white porcelain of the sink. Lots of them.

She woke that night in the dark, the faint mewling again, the side of her face, tight. Sticking to the pillow. In the bathroom half her face was a mask of blood. She hadn't had a nose bleed since she was a child. Her mother's slap. She imagined the spiders. Disappeared down the sink in the underworld of drains and pipes now lurking, grown so big. But they would have died by now, anyway. And they weren't real in the first place. Nothing lived, down there.

It was small, mottled brown. It circled around the room at mad speed, wings beating, and smashed into the glass door. It dropped to the floor, stunned, and lay twitching. No one else moved. She stepped over toward the door, to open it. One dark eye watched her, flickering. The other was bloody. With the energy of panic the bird struggled, gained air and battered repeatedly against the glass, leaving a smear, then fell again. Too exhausted to escape it lay crumpled on the floor. She picked it up. Cupped in her hands she felt its heart stop, felt the frantic life escape. She stood holding it. It seemed like ages. Someone took it out of her hands. She didn't notice who. She brushed tears from her cheeks with the back of her hand and stepped outside.

The ringing phone was incessant. She snatched it up, "Hello?"

"Miss Carter?" There was something snide in the woman's voice. "Westbourne Women's Health Clinic. It's about your appointment on Thursday the 17th. We have to cancel…"

"My appointment was last month. The 17th. Last month."

"We won't have to cancel, then." Then there was just a harsh mechanical clicking in her ear from the disconnected line, almost like laughter.

She remembered Scott's mother, but not Scott, only the thing he'd become. She was standing under the white mulberry tree, thick with fruit like pale mauve grubs, when his mother drove in from the poppy covered hillside. Fields of pale purple flowers. They grew them, under a government licence, for the pharmaceutical industry, and some for blue poppy seeds for bakeries. His mother wore a straw hat, a straw coloured dress, painted wooden clogs. She was brown and creased from too much labour, too much sun. She dragged the matted brown corpse of an animal by the leg out of the tray of the pick-up truck, and dumped it at her feet. "Tasmanian Devil. They're dying out, cancer." Emma understood she meant it as a kind of nature study, a local curiosity, but there was something primal about it, something disturbing.

Then Scott was there, tut tutting, and saying "Mother," but she could only remember the skeletal thing he'd become. She saw it saying "Mother, Emma doesn't want to see that." It was only two weeks later he was too exhausted to move, and barely a month again, a wasted, incoherent, skeletal thing.

She couldn't carry that with her, so she left it. She wasn't there at the end, but it wasn't Scott. The thought of it made her feel infected. She certainly couldn't carry its baby.

But now her belly was swollen, aching. There was something inside her. Something savage. Gnawing. An ugly red spider. A dead bird. With Scott's withered heart, and the teeth of a strange animal. A devil.

The window was blue, purity, the sun a promise of warmth. But she could see herself all broken on the pavement but the thing still inside her, feeding. Jagged pain, claws that had been skittering suddenly insistent. On the drum-tight skin of her distended belly, dragging welts.

She took the cold steel handle, its curve so elegant, the geometry of its blade so harsh by comparison, a hard white triangle, she saw the guts spill out glistening, something red, something yellow, something black from the belly of the animal as Scott's mother ran a small knife down its side.

In the bathroom she grasped the towel rail for support, warm damp cloth and cold steel under her fingers. As she took a stance, adjusted her grip on the knife, turning it inwards, put her other hand to her belly, lifted, she felt a brief caress on her palm, almost tender.

She thought of tea and white hands as the blade went in. A confusion of cutting and scrabbling, her chest heaving. The white pain was a relief, the pressure dissolved. It fell out of her onto the porcelain floor tiles in a wash of blood. It was a thing, all red. Spindly tentacular arms, writhing, skittering. Glistening and bulbous. It left a trail where it crawled. Its mewling pierced her ears. It slithered to the toilet, its appendages lashing, crawled up, slid over the seat.

Emma could hear it call, as she ran, stumbled, staggered, dragged to the window. She could feel the red spiders below the earth, their awareness, a sudden demand.

The air pricked the sweat on her face. She felt the sun for a moment.

Mist swirls and clears, revealing an elaborate hearse, all ebon wood and brass finials and railings, bearing within glass panelled sides, a small white coffin, surrounded by flowers, preternaturally bright in the fog of pre-dawn.

The horse, in its traces, is of the pantomime variety. Baggy skinned, cartoonishly dappled, and wearing a crumpled top hat, its bent ears poking through the brim.

Leaning against the tall spoked wheel of the carriage. Still, shadowy figures.

The dawn brightens, a glow grey through the slowly thinning mist reveals stones and statuary, rising serried rows, diverse but orderly. Upon the hill, the yellow claw-headed shape of a digging machine. Distant, beyond bordering pines, the outlines of carnival structures, a Ferris Wheel, and other less familiar machinery, shadowed, still and stark upon the horizon.

The sky the colour of the space between dreams brightens of a sudden. The two figures are revealed. Pink faced in the cold, much of a muchness. Resplendent in funereal confection. Gleaming black ribbons. Tall silk top hats. Kid gloves. Pressed three-quarter coats. No more, no less. Vests trousers shoes. Black on black on black. Even their eyes like polished coal.

Black strings, almost invisible, extend from our poor players, up into the infinite.

"And today?" Asks Edgar.

"The quieted machinery of joy" says Samuel. He drops a fag end to the ground. Grinds it under the toe of a gleaming leather shoe. Gravel scrapes. Birds hush for a moment.

"And today," he says, in a voice neither here nor there.

"Today we bury a child," says Edgar. He turns up his collar, against the cold, for a moment. For propriety he turns it down again.

"Hm." A sudden gust soughs through the silent moment.

"The trees, the way they are swayed and whispered by the wind, and suddenly still, do you not find it...fearful and ominous?"

Edgar's voice is also quieted.

"I have no fear of them" says Samuel, matter-of-factly.

"You have been at this work too long, then, if you do not find, on a morning when we bury a child, that the noble pines and bent-statured oaks grieve the sadness of the wind."

"No. No. It is not that I am inured past mystery, so wearied by routine that I am dumb to the significance, so read, so spoken. It is only, I am grown beyond fearing."

"So you are an old soldier," says Edgar, and in voice fading "bloodshed has you death's maid of honour, laying the mudded train of earth upon those who wed the great polygamer, in requiem for the nameless, the faceless, left at the altar by the dissolute avowal of your rifle."

"I was a soldier, yes." replies Samuel. "I left I do not know how many unknown, unburied, open eyed yet sightless to the sky. But those I inter today I do not bury in recompense to the unburied of yesteryear. I have known killing but I do not know death."

"Today we bury a child. Grievous," says Edgar. He shakes his head. "The trees cry. You will not respect and fear."

Samuel nods. "We all know the shell game is a trick, but the many of us still choose to be deceived."

"A hero of wars past, who, in his wisdom no longer gambles," says Edgar, perhaps with a respectful sarcasm.

"No" says Samuel. And again, "No. Before the war, I suffered grande mal. The seizures would throw me to the earth, trembling. I thought, then, that was like death." (A pause of denial.) "After the war, I do not know by what vicissitudes, for I suffered not the slightest physical wound, at a time when I was responsible for, well, one shell game or another, I experienced a seizure in which I no longer trembled, I no longer swooned as of death. I feared. A fear gripped my ankles, my viscera, my throat. I ran until I could not. Feaar. Blinding, sweating, adrenal. You understand? Lacking any object of terror with which the mind could even begin to grapple. The site of my epilepsy had altered to where reside the base emotions, the temporal lobe. I knew fear, white hot and unconscionable."

"You must have known it was the epilepsy...your previous experience," suggested Edgar.

"It happened thrice before I realised."

"Thrice!"

"Thrice" says Samuel, (with finality, then a pause.)

"I cannot recall the experiences to you."

"You lived then, in fear of the fear."

"The fear of the fear was a harbinger, a goad, a constant, ominous foreshadow of the unreckoned force of the moment of seizure."

"So now?"

"I was prescribed henbane, witch hazel, widow's reckon, laudanum. Later, other drugs. They weakened and wearied my body, my youth. The potential of recurrence tormented me, mind and soul. I spent years, how many, I no longer know, in fear of fear."

"You are no more in fear of fear," says Edgar, a conclusion like straw.

"I turned to the grave-work, at first perhaps, driven by the necessity of a choice; to escape or endure. I was wracked then. Gluttonous with heat and venom and night. In these memorious gardens, amongst the many, remembered only in moments, only as ciphers of moments, and for that, perhaps, unremembered but in stillness, yet speaking, a solemnity, calming as autumn evening, settled upon me. I chose, and stopped the medication. Soon thereafter I strengthened, in body, in spirit. The fear had cauterised the epilepsy, the epilepsy the fear."

"You without fear. These interred ciphers, as you call them, silent in sepulchres. Speaking only in remembered voices or the deceit of speech given them on living tongues. Without the respect, the godly respect, born of fear, the lives they speak through memory become the acts and dialogues of poppets, of marionettes. You must fear and offer due respect."

"You presume to know fear? Your strings are showing. This fearing you suppose invokes respect is no more than the cowering of a cur before its master, of a man before his. It is to placate the living, to submit obeisance to every institute that holds him, that he erroneously holds as his. It is to play of their lives a shell game, in which choice is denied, the prize is palmed, they are judged ill or good, summarily sentenced nevertheless. This respect is more ignorant than death. I do not call the dead, for dead men tell no tales, nor honour them, but give them peace which is their due. Beyond fear, how can I do otherwise?"

(A pause, the men stretch, yawn and gaze around.)

"The day warms." says Edgar.

"Forgive my momentary tone of anger, to speak in defence of the unvoiced, is a challenge to which my passion rises."

"It is understandable. In debate, strong words are exchanged and easily forgotten. Your undertaking is indeed a challenge; for, truly, is not to speak for another, to speak their voice as your own, the unvoiced cannot speak. Your words have not been spoken."

"Perhaps, I have not spoken my words."

"Nor theirs."

(Both feign ignorance of the others' presence, for a moment, adjusting the fine black strings, glinting in the brightening day, that rise vertically from knee, wrist and head, into the blue.)

"Who then is speaking," says Samuel.

"Who is speaking?" asks Edgar.

"Who speaks?" enquires Samuel.

"Speaks?" Edgar

"Who?"

Both laugh.

Edgar acknowledges with a gloved hand the conveyance within the bedecked and glassed carriage. He says, jaw clacking, "This one. The coffin was made small. The mother could not pay for another. The mortician broke the child's legs to cramp her in the box. There is little peace in that."

"Still flesh knows no discomfort. Yet here we are with all our finery. Do you find peace in gravework?"

"Ah, so so. It is work as much as prayer is labour. I am diligent and respectful in both. Formerly, I have slaughtered, I have butchered, I have worked motor lines, I have driven public conveyances. I am concerned of the news and pray for the starving. I feast on the sabbath. I honour my wife and do not understand my children. It is life, goodly ordered. Quarter of a half, half of a quarter."

"I wonder for whom the wind grieves. Sometimes it seems the living more than the dead."

"Once I too was a doubter. I doubted all things, and lived in uncertainty. I suppose it was doubt lead me to this work, where I found the inevitable."

"Now you are sure, Edgar?"

"As the sky is blue. Certain."

"Then you were certain of your uncertainty?"

"This is excess – , all bridled and relenting. What a way of speaking!"

"Calm, calm. It is certainly beyond doubt that you were in doubt."

"Well, I suppose that must be, for in doubting doubt, it would leave open that I was not in doubt, which was certainly not so."

"Doubtless. A possibility as open, as welcoming and as certain as the grave," concludes Samuel.

Now your strings are showing."

"Pardon," says Samuel.

With a flourish, a flight of doves from his sleeves, his strings are gone, but for a glimmer.

They look to the distance, don their hats then proceed to open the carriage doors.

"Hold. The procession comes. This morning we bury a child."

"It is time. The sun is well risen."

You are all born of the miscegenation of too correspondent flesh.

First, I paint my face before a warped mirror.
Done, I smile, I tie on my mask.

I am dead.
I am dead.
My face is masked in web.

I do not remember ever being young.

When I was of that particular age at which awareness of self becomes a burgeoning crisis, I became intensely concerned with a scar, which, for reasons then unknown to me, but which I now ascribe to pain, had remained outside my conscious recognition.

The scar curved down my right side, conversely and beneath the curve of the smooth flesh of my belly, and vanished between the top of my thigh and my groin.

The scar was like the thin red lips of an ageing hag, pursed together and silenced by thick black stitches.

I asked my mother about the scar and she said I had had an operation when I was two to remove my appendix which was infested with maggots.

Seeing my droopy eyes and crimson spotted cheeks and broad smile reflected in the blankness of a television screen, I forgot about the scar, and for some weeks so wanted to become Luna Park, whose grinning portal I had seen in a news story about a fire in the Ghost Train, which had incinerated a young family. For that horror Luna Park was closed, and I knew I could never become Luna Park, despite the scar that rollercoasted across my belly.

I could hear the hag grumbling and whispering behind her sewn together lips, keeping me awake at nights, and I became convinced that if only I could undo the stitches, she would speak, telling me the secrets of the Ghost Train and the Grinning Face.

However, I was quite in horror of the hag, despite her whispered promises, and it was some weeks before I was brave enough to take my father's razor and my mother's tweezers from the medicine cabinet, and open with them my own flesh.

Taking the razor, I cut away the translucent, pearly skin that had grown over the first stitch, then dug at it, and got a hold of it with the tweezers and pulled. Lifting the tweezers to my nose, I sniffed the stitch, which smelled of decaying roses, then finding no place to put it, I placed it between my lips and swallowed. This I continued, leaving a bloody track down my side.

Tracing the slippery scar all the way down with my forefinger, which I had never previously done, I discovered that it was stitched all the way behind my scrotum, almost to my anus.

No longer using the tweezers, but pulling at the stitches behind my scrotum with my fingers, I finally found the hag's lips, which swelled and opened.

She sucked on my fingers as her voice welled inside me, and my penis suddenly grew hard, which sickened her, because she was vomiting then, and my fingers were all sticky with blood and the juices spurting up from inside me and out my balls and my stiff penis. And then I fainted.

Much later, which now is quite recently, I checked the medical records at the hospital where I was born, learning that I was born an hermaphrodite, and that when it was medically feasible, at around the age of two, my womb and ovaries had been removed.

My hormonal balance must have been disturbed, because soon after the operation I began having erections whenever my flesh contacted another's. My parents, I suppose, were too embarrassed to take me back to the hospital to finish sealing my vagina.

What most angered the hag inside me, though, when I learned of the operation, was that the surgeon had removed from me a perfectly healthy appendix.

The old woman inside me, whom I came to know as La Luna, (although that is not her name) and I spoke often, and she told me all of women's secrets.

Although I was reluctant, La Luna insisted I return to the hospital and destroy records of both my birth and my operation.

There, I was prevented from completing my task by a surgeon, (whose name is not Natalie but whom I shall call Natalie) who was researching some case histories with regard to the separation of Siamese Twins.

I called her Butcher, a term of endearment by which I had known a fellow employee at the abattoir at which I was previously employed, and began to tell her of my operation, but La Luna began drooling and speaking up inside me and told me to say;

Stop for a moment, and look at my face: it is in animation that the human face is perceived as possessed of beauty. In moments of stillness, in repose, devoid of the traits and quirks of practiced charismatics, the human face presents its unmasked aspect; and that is so ugly, and that is so ugly, my face is masked in web.

But that of course is so judgemental, and in judgement I hold to the opposite, but it is some while since I have become beyond judgement.

The horror of my contempt excited Natalie to an aweful aspect, and she invited me to return to her apartment to discuss the butchery of my excised appendix, which was purely a pretext.

Travelling by taxi to her apartment, I amused Natalie by reciting a poem composed for my former co-worker at the Municipal Abattoir, entitled

Red Meat

My cleavered love she knows
so well how to CUT.
Butcher me gently my lovely

in our house of charnel joys.
Clotted walls built to the measure
of her preserving cold
searing as a brand
ugly am i as cattle
to the slaughter
lowing in ex pec tation.
Eyes the vaults of wisdom as blunt,
her cursing tongue as blind as the blade
more vacant than her eyes
rolled to whites of orgasm
shrieking, "Because I won't fuck you!"
Because you always fuck me
over and falling i just fill with my sense
oblivious to the perpetuity of the jags
of the stems of roses dried black
and watch the screaming as the cutter cuts,
reeling in the wealth
of my trebizond anaesthesia.

At Natalie's apartment, I matched her pretext with my postext, saying, "When the Butcher, whom I wrote that poem for, was tense, I'd massage her neck and shoulders," and Natalie sat on the couch between my legs and I gripped her thighs with my thighs and began to massage her tight shoulders, continuing, "One day, after our shift, she'd just changed out of her coverall, and I touched her shoulders and she swung around and her fist cracked on my mouth, and tasting the blood I couldn't help but laugh, and laughing, I sprayed her white shirt with blood and she reached up with her hands like wither pink butterflies to wipe the blood away but couldn't because her small pointy breasts with nipples as erect as Eiffel Towers were pressing tight against the flourine white shimmer of her blood spattered shirt, and seeing two of my teeth embedded in the bleeding wound on the back of her hand, her eyes rolled to whites of orgasm and she fainted. Later she cut their heads off, baked some, boiled others. Served all glistening with a red wine and honey sauce."

I massaged Natalie for three quarters of an hour, her shoulders first, because a woman's tender memory is in her shoulders, then the juncture of her neck and jaw, her shoulder blades as she wriggled out of her blouse, her spine, her back, the crescent of flesh beneath her breasts, all the while whispering,

You are the engine you are the train
You are the fire you are the steel
You are the cauldron you are the steam
You are the piston you are the rail
You are the brakeman you are the screams
You are the iron you are the sinew
Take this lapse of bone and fire
You will be the Ghost Train
Ten thousand tons of steel
Pistons breaking bones
Damning fire damned wheels
All the hungry ghosts
All the broken skulls
Mercy broken bridges

I shall be that cavern
Cut from the mountain
With broken bones
All the fallen bridges
Every fallen stone
Moraine and morass
Every landslide
Breaks the line
Wet and dark
Rank and cold
Grace and anger
The cut the anguish
You are the feast
I am the famine
I am the blood
You are the bone
All that hot and broken iron
All those known destinies
On rigid lines
You are the Ghost Train
Mahogany and glass
Staining the upholstery
Burning breath expelled
Across vocal folds
The master of the graves
Shakes the cemetery earth
To liquefaction
Corruption pours away
Undermined
Undetermined
Undestined

Come into me hollow
I am the thrum of the track
You are the suicidal cavalry attack
The wreck
The kamikaze
The concrete collapse
I am the dereliction
The ghost the haunt and the ellipse
I am the umbrage
You are the crucifixion
I am the tunnel of love

until her breathing quickened and shallowed and her blood pulsed and she became as malleable as cotton candy, soft as river clay down which my hands slid so I pressed the base of her spine in three hard circular pulses, La Luna vomiting inside me, Natalie in orgasm, her thighs shaking her vagina opening vastly as she slid to the floor her legs open her juices wetting the crutch of her slacks, so that she cried that she wanted more and La Luna screamed fuck me fuck me fuck me until my teeth clenched and I shouted, this is not about ffffucking, this is not about ffffffucking, *my face is masked in web.*

And Natalie put her fingers under her belt to wet them with her dew and her blood because it was her period, and thrusting her fingers into my mouth, her blood, honey and the split flesh of Siamese Twins, I said "If you will wear a phallus and fuck me I will give you all that you desire" and Natalie was screaming "I WON'T FUCK YOU!" And La Luna was gaping and screaming and vomiting her hot vomit so to silence them all like the healer of some false faith I pushed my fingertips into the soft flesh of her back so the flesh split, and grasped her womb, crushing it in my fingers and jerked it out so she was all blood, she was all blood, my face is masked in web.

I do not hate you.
I do not love you.

One day you shall see me, waiting to cross the road or sitting in a cafe in the brightness of day and I will ask, "Do you have the time?" or "Do you know the way to Orwell Street?" or some such other innocuous query, and you shall answer, because, perhaps, you will see Luna Park in my droopy eyes or my rosy cheeks or my broad grin and you shall smile and answer, or you shall frown and answer, and will not recognise me.

I wish that my words would kill you but they kill only a little, so with my hands, or with a knife, or driving a fast moving car as mad as a rollercoaster, I will follow and I will find you, just to show the person you call yourself, whether you call yourself man, whether you call yourself woman, and allow your fellow man to burst his flesh into you, whether you prefer a woman's manly ministrations or blooding the loins of children, La Luna will purse her lips, and pout, and open her mouth to vomit and to scream and you shall not hear her, you shall not hear her.

> *I am dead.*
> *I am dead.*
> *My face is masked in web.*

Wessex Cyclotron he calls asylum, and for Wessex Cyclotron he works. Wessex Cyclotron do work for government, and so contracted, his precious time, he entertains the bourgeois sons and daughters of the Government University of Technology, to which Wessex is attached. GUT he calls asylum too, for entirely other reasons. His students he is supposed to entertain with his presence, a speaking monkey, but instead entertains with video:

The grey monitor lizard nuzzles the parched carcass of the wallaby. The digitised images shudder and pull out of shape, he is white-hot and the radiation of the screen sucks into his arms and chest. His face, hollow eyes, sharp cheekbones undercut by the lines of his beard is reflected, while stable remains a ghost.) Dust and flies cloud. The lizard tears into the taut flesh across the rib cage. Entrails spill out, moist and purple. The monitor with a single sideways motion rips the maggot scarred viscera, raises its head to the violet evening, tendrils of flesh hanging from its lips, and swallows. The low sun negatives in that silhouette.

He thumbs audio edit and lays the sonore, whitened with static, of voice over

"Like the slamming together of plutonium rod and plutonium jill, in the first instance following the colossal hiatus that enacted the universe, that entity consisted of a seething, writhing ejaculation of photinos, neutrinos, gravitinos, quarks and an extinct cosmogeny of exotic hi-energy particles. Out of that sea condensed the light-matter of which the universe is copulated. The mass of that light-matter does not account for the gravitation that maintains the tenuity of galaxies, and of galactic clusters, from flying asunder.

There must exist, therefore, an unseen matter, whose gravity holds and accounts; dark matter.

The gravitational force required of dark-matter to maintain galactic clusters and thus the universe itself has reached beyond the point of force at which the collapse of the universe should have occurred. Space is either tensed as stretched wire (or snapped, and we on the periphery merely in wait of the full force of recoil) otherwise dark-matter must follow a compensatory process of decay. Constituted as a balance relative to the universal point of origin, any attempt to create the conditions of existence, or to synthesise dark-matter, is an absolute transgression.

Betwixt the condensation of the constituitive entirety, into points of light darkness was pulled into being; for less than vacuum cannot exist; and the ratio of that dark to light is nine to one.

Maintaining and dominating the universe, in all its binding gravity, is this dark-matter: the darkest, for even light is bound thereby. We are left to pose the question: is it in the tension between conjunction and the tearing and rending of matter that darkness is created?"

The low sun negatives in that

silhouette.

Hypnotic

He thumbs the edit-title and a bold sans-serif text is screened

ASTROPHYSICS FOR BEGINNERS
by
Dr John St Devine

These words melt, like acid in flesh.

He placed the recording in the out tray for the substitute, and came into the raw broken dawn.

All that day he sat lotus in the sun. His eyes stung with sweat, and he ignored them, watching the pulse in the crimson film of his eyelids. The sweat trickled through his beard so it was glistening and wet. A colleague questioned him.

"Exposure," he said, and his colleague said "Oh" and shrugged and departed. The sun of noon burned his face, and he forgot it. His thin lips cracked and bled. The breeze of evening cooled him and he rose up, hollow and swollen when finally darkness descended and the lights of the city livened its shadows.

The staff apartment furnishings and fixtures were built for a people smaller than himself, and that unnerved him.

He showered, the water so hot it scalded his red flesh redder. He shaved, then swiped a flannel across the steam clouded mirror. He sneered at the face in that rivulet trickling slash. A high-browed, sun-burned grinning red skull face.

The red death, he thought. And dressed in a green nearest black silk suit then descended to be amongst the other shadows of the city floor. And the shadows bent around him, as he walked and he thought that homage.

The sign over the graffiti scarred door read, *The Fuck Club* in violet neon.

The light within was red, and the flesh. He felt anonymous in that light, amongst that flesh. He kissed the soft mouth of a pale beautiful manboy, and the hot breath of that mouth tasted of jism and milk and vomit, and that made him hard.

The boy said, "I might suck your cock if it's nice, then again I might not. Maybe I just want you to suck mine. I won't be fucked up the arse, though. My arse is too delicate for that."

"Envious cunt," said the Red Death. "I hate you so much I want to come in your face." And he hit the boy hard with the base of a beer bottle, so the boy's face broke and became ugly with blood. Then he was beaten himself and cast into the street.

A girl looked down on him, *Corona Borealis* in her eyes, plush lips black under the violet. She knelt and with the corner of her chiffon dress touched the dark from his split lip.

"I'm a nursing sister," she said, "I work in pathology. I infect myself with strains of dangerous flu viruses, so I'm ill and my brow and palms sweat. On Saturday mornings I walk around in shopping malls giving coins from my hands to old people and small children. Unless they are strong, they die."

"I am beyond strength but need your help," he said.

They take a black cab to Wessex.

Outside the glass doors of the laboratories, while he waits to override security access, he looks into the glitter of her eyes, the snow of her face. He touches the fine white silk of her, massages with two fingers the juncture of jaw and neck behind her ear. Two thin black hairs, curled as a knave's moustache hang out her nostril. She inhales and they withdraw. Her plush lips open a breath, as if she prepares for a tentative kiss. A crimson and emerald wasp spits out. Another emerges out her nostril, pauses, tasting the dew of her lip then hums electric with the first around the white hemisphere of the overhead light. Her mouth opens wide, and she speaks while another and another spits out of her, "In a different permutation the same chemical as makes emeralds green, rubies red." Her eyes gape and she vomits a static-crackling swarm of the wasps.

Their legion massed and dripping, darkens the dome of the light. The shriek of them shatters the glass, its fragments fall. Redgreen luminance transluces.

The door slides open and their footsteps crack stutter through the corridors.

In the ante-room, amidst panels and glows, he instructs her on which lever to pull, and which button to impress, when he was prepared, and signalled. He stripped and she folded and hung his clothes. Then she fed him a handful of lubricant gel.

In the Target Chamber he sank into mantra and pranayama, asana (the dragon) dharana and dhyana.

She in the ante-room paused to consider her actions, then slid-to the lever that lowered the gold-plated lead chain.

In the Target Chamber he, sat as the dragon, took the end of the lowering chain into his mouth. It tasted of acid warm and fizzing cola. He opened his tract and slowly swallowed, as a snake swallowing a snake. When a metre of gold hung like a chain tail out his anus he reached back and grasped it, and raising his arm clipped the end to the chain above him.

In the ante-room, watching the monitor, she returned the lever that hoisted the chain. He hung suspended, the base of an illumined scalene. His legs dangled, his arms wide.

As man in flight, she thought.

He gently swayed. Sweat dripped from the nipples, erect on his outstretched chest. Fluid from the tip of his erection traced a silver thread to the floor. He stared into the vanishing point of the curving away tunnel of the particle accelerator and felt through him: the universe too is curved.

She watched the monitor, pulsed the button.

The hair of his head and his body writhed. His face glowed. His eyes bled. The gaze of the eyes of the universe beheld him. Ions smashed through the gold hurled it to fragments, exotic hi-energy **LIVING ION COSMOGENY** hurled off the lead smashed out through **HE UNIVERSE** his body spasmed

SAMHADI

he ejaculated, shots of black *betwist that condensation darkness is pulled into being.*

His erection grew flaccid, and the chain above him snapped and he fell heavy to the floor. He lay still, curled and foetal. She considered leaving, but couldn't leave him that.

In the Target Chamber, the sound of her weeping woke him. She helped him disembogue the length of chain. His eyes, his mouth were black.

They returned through the corridors towards the night. Tufts and drifts of her hair fell to her shoulders. Her teeth loosened, cracked, crumbled, fell. Her skin writhed and tightened. Her bones ached like passions. As they passed a mirrored door, she saw herself; become hag. And maddened, clung to his back and clawed at his face. He ran, hagridden, and his footsteps star-shattered the tile.

A klaxon of alarm pulsed its intonation, but she had died before quarantine doors had sealed them.

Police in contamination suits prised her from him with crowbars, and bagged and cased her broken remnants.

He was bagged and cased and trucked and revelled in the night of it.

His trial was for her murder. To it he was brought from the night of an armoured leaden vault, in an armoured leaden transport, his gravity restrained, his mobility ordered by a steel exo-skeleta. His gravity broke the frame, broke the dock, broke the bench. The jury was the world, and the jury delighted the spectacle.

The judge summarised,

"Some say the essence of the law is justice. Yet some transgressions go beyond what can be hung on justice's scales and still balanced. The state of vacuum to nature is abhorrent. What goes beyond vacuum, morte so. Neither church nor state nor reason will tolerate, if nature will not, that abhorrence. You have brought into order, chaos, where there should only be order. For that the only fit punishment is to be hung to your death by the gravity of your own offence.

Have you final words?"

"The law is that which maps transgression, and then bans repetition and repetition of permutation of those transgressions. It is law, searching for new acts to ban that drives forward to the next. It is law that with a force as inexorable as gravity moves from arson to assualt, rape to murder, mass murder, genocide, holocaust. Every genre of offence is necessary and permitted to the Law. It is the individual act which goes beyond law, and must be recorded exactly, banned, and finalised with death."

But his gravity turned his words, so the judge, the jury, all thought he said

"I will rip my way through the flesh of this earth"

"Your descent shall be unpredescented," said the judge and signed the death warrant. And the sleeve of his robe effaced the ink of his own signing.

The carcass was to be delivered into space.

With celebration as of carnival or auto de fe, he was trucked to a cell on the cement planed and buffered and bunkered field, at the base of the rocket scaffold, a device of pulleys, block, tackle, gear and counterweight, had been constructed.

Broken from the exo-skeleta, its fragments clinging to him, he rested till his mass cracked the concrete of the floor. He sat on a steel bunk and its tubes twisted and bent around him. When momently unobserved, he snapped a thirty centimetre length of railing tube, tipped up his head and swallowed so it walled his throat.

The noose was steel cable for strength, enclosed in Virginia hemp, wound about with thirteen turns and thrice knotted for tradition.

He was taken up, and the height of it giddied the men around him, so they sweated in their contamination suits. A priest was present.

"Have you last words of repentance, my son?"

He opened his mouth and a sound, hollow as of the sea in a conch, breathed out. The priest looked into his black eyes and turned away his face.

"*Ego te absolvo?*" whispered the priest, and thought, "*Ego te...*"

Hydraulic manipules bagged his head. The knot was tightened to the juncture of jaw and neck behind his ear. The steel of the trap quaked under his feet. The descent was full of chaos and the glory of existence, a mutual force beyond any denial. The jerk snapped and he span as a gyroscope, the rope describing the generatrix of a cone.

After he had spun for hours and the condensation of matter upon him began the first storming elements and electrics of an ecology, the centrifugal governor was disengaged. The rope tightened and he spun a radical orbit, smashing the scaffold brace so it bent around him and the structure tumbled.

Rubble, debris, detritus fell from him. Amongst the wreckage his body was still. The warder and hangman removed the noose from his neck and the bag from his head. They saw how the rope had cut into his throat, and the blackness of his blood. No pulse, no heart. The doctor declared him dead. The priest refused last rites. The orderly wrapped him in a lead winding sheet.

Between the broken scaffold and the laboratory where he would be examined, analysed, prepared for space, he disembogued the steel pipe into his hand. He clubbed the warder, the hangman, the orderly, the doctor, so their skulls inside their masks burst.

The priest cowered, and he left him to his own insense.

Driving the ambulance he escaped the field into the city night.

A tall, leather clad man looked into his face outside the red door of a club called the Pumping Room. The man's eyes lusted with fear, and he passed him by, entering the red door. Young people danced under pulsing coloured lights, their bodies jerking in parodies of fucking. He drew their sweat about him, and it tasted to his flesh as of the sweetly impure dew of their Eden.

A dark skinned girl with Elizabeth Taylor eyes and Persian jewellery said to him something he didn't hear and giggled.

He shook his head and she spoke again,

"Now see that noble and most sovereign reason,
Like sweet bells jangled, out of tune and harsh;
That unmatched form and feature of blown youth..."
"Blasted with ecstasy. O woe is me
To have seen what I have seen, see what I see!
I would lay you on your belly on white silk sheets
and lift your arse in the air and slowly slide
inside you, to feel your cunt devouring my cock,
your buttocks rolling pressed by my hips.
At the point of absolute devourment
I'll push your face into the pillow until you're smothered
and your ragged breathing stops."
"The economy of night is an economy of darkness.
The economy of darkness is the economy of desire;
a force as inexorable as gravity.
Behind the soft folds of my cunt's lips,
is barbed wire for your cock."
"Most desire that, other than which they cannot have."
"I desire all that there is."

On the subway to GUT they watched as a group of stockbrokers beat to death a sloe-eyed youth.

In the apartment, while her gravity broken body cooled on the bed, the Red Death drew the curtains wide and stood back, looking into his mask in the city dark and city light smeared glass. He ran the few steps in great powerful strides and leapt, pushing his face into his face, so he penetrated and the virginal glass fractured around him.

His descent was unpredescented. His gravity retarded time, accelerated light to blackness. He fell, tumbling ten to the sixth years approaching c.

Fall forever describing the universe curve and spin a spiral tangent, along the wave of the dynamic ribbon he extruded, in continually altered repetition. The cold air burned and the shadows of the night bent around him. There was nadir future, perpetuous present, eternal recursion, peak of the continuous wave, whose future is past continuously permuting at relativistic rates.

Oblivion went out him.

Softened he was broken on the hard steel edge of a waste disposal bin. All his body busted, but he lay twisted and crumpled amongst the spilled garbage and the livened shadows of the city night, twitching until dawn, when a dog came and ate part of his entrails. The dog walked away and vomited. Flies laid their eggs in his guts, and when the man from the waste collection service found him, he swore he saw a red lizard crawling in the hollow of the man's belly, along his spine, and out his anus.

There is something red on the lawn.

It glistens below the sycamore tree. There is something red on the lawn.

Coarse, bristling nettles. It glistens below the sycamore tree. There is something red on the lawn.

A little green showing through. Coarse, bristling nettles. It glistens below the sycamore tree. There is something red on the lawn.

The grass dried to yellow. A little green showing through. Coarse, bristling nettles. It glistens below the sycamore tree. There is something red on the lawn.

The yard is an expanse of hard baked earth. The grass dried to yellow. A little green showing through. Coarse, bristling nettles. It glistens below the sycamore tree. There is something red on the lawn.

The porch rail juts in disarray, splayed like finger bones. The yard is an expanse of hard baked earth. The grass dried to yellow. A little green showing through. Coarse, bristling nettles. It glistens below the sycamore tree. There is something red on the lawn.

Behind rotted vines, through cracked panes, grey lace made white a moment in the failing sun of the still evening. The porch rail juts in disarray, splayed like finger bones. The yard is an expanse of hard baked earth. The grass dried to yellow. A little green showing through. Coarse, bristling nettles. It glistens below the sycamore tree. There is something red on the lawn.

Shadows. Behind rotted vines, through cracked panes, grey lace made white a moment in the failing sun of the still evening. The porch rail juts in disarray, splayed like finger bones. The yard is an expanse of hard baked earth. The grass dried to yellow. A little green showing through. Coarse, bristling nettles. It glistens below the sycamore tree. There is something red on the lawn.

The cicadas silent. Shadows. Behind rotted vines, through cracked panes, grey lace made white a moment in the failing sun of the still evening. The porch rail juts in disarray, splayed like finger bones. The yard is an expanse of hard baked earth. The grass dried to yellow. A little green showing through. Coarse, bristling nettles. It glistens below the sycamore tree. There is something red on the lawn.

The doors askew, jagged on broken hinges. The cicadas silent. Shadows. Behind rotted vines, through cracked panes, grey lace made white a moment in the failing sun of the still evening. The porch rail juts in disarray, splayed like finger bones. The yard is an expanse of hard baked earth. The grass dried to yellow. A little green showing through. Coarse, bristling nettles. It glistens below the sycamore tree. There is something red on the lawn.

Dust white in the gloom on wrenched stairs. The doors askew, jagged on broken hinges. The cicadas silent. Shadows. Behind rotted vines, through cracked panes, grey lace made white a moment in the failing sun of the still evening. The porch rail juts in disarray, splayed like finger bones. The yard is an expanse of hard baked earth. The grass dried to yellow. A little green showing through. Coarse, bristling nettles. It glistens below the sycamore tree. There is something red on the lawn.

Glass scattered, aglitter, stars on night's shore. Dust white in the gloom on wrenched stairs. The doors askew, jagged on broken hinges. The cicadas silent. Shadows. Behind rotted vines, through cracked panes, grey lace made white a moment in the failing sun of the still evening. The porch rail juts in disarray, splayed like finger bones. The yard is an expanse of hard baked earth. The grass dried to yellow. A little green showing through. Coarse, bristling nettles. It glistens below the sycamore tree. There is something red on the lawn.

A cloud encroaches. Glass scattered, aglitter, stars on night's shore. Dust white in the gloom on wrenched stairs. The doors askew, jagged on broken hinges. The cicadas silent. Shadows. Behind rotted vines, through cracked panes, grey lace made white a moment in the failing sun of the still evening. The porch rail juts in disarray, splayed like finger bones. The yard is an expanse of hard baked earth. The grass dried to yellow. A little green showing through. Coarse, bristling nettles. It glistens below the sycamore tree. There is something red on the lawn.

A cloud encroaches. Glass scattered, aglitter, stars on night's shore. Dust white in the gloom on wrenched stairs. The doors askew, jagged on broken hinges. The cicadas silent. Shadows. Behind rotted vines, through cracked panes, grey lace made white a moment in the failing sun of the still evening. The porch rail juts in disarray, splayed like finger bones. The yard is an expanse of hard baked earth. The grass dried to yellow. A little green showing through. Coarse, bristling nettles. It glistens below the sycamore tree. There is something red on the lawn.

Ashes drift, hesitant, a cold exhalation from the maw of broke, scorched, tumbledown boards. A cloud encroaches. Glass scattered, aglitter, stars on night's shore. Dust white in the gloom on wrenched stairs. The doors askew, jagged on broken hinges. The cicadas silent. Shadows. Behind rotted vines, through cracked panes, grey lace made white a moment in the failing sun of the still evening. The porch rail juts in disarray, splayed like finger bones. The yard is an expanse of hard baked earth. The grass dried to yellow. A little green showing through. Coarse, bristling nettles. It glistens below the sycamore tree. There is something red on the lawn.

Dark turns. Ashes drift, hesitant, a cold exhalation from the maw of broke, scorched, tumbledown boards. A cloud encroaches. Glass scattered, aglitter, stars on night's shore. Dust white in the gloom on wrenched stairs. The doors askew, jagged on broken hinges. The cicadas silent. Shadows. Behind rotted vines, through cracked panes, grey lace made white a moment in the failing sun of the still evening. The porch rail juts in disarray, splayed like finger bones. The yard is an expanse of hard baked earth. The grass dried to yellow. A little green showing through. Coarse, bristling nettles. It glistens below the sycamore tree. There is something red on the lawn.

In the ash, the grey, the burnt lace, the glitter. Dark turns. Ashes drift, hesitant, a cold exhalation from the maw of broke, scorched, tumbledown boards. A cloud encroaches. Glass scattered, aglitter, stars on night's shore. Dust white in the gloom on wrenched stairs. The doors askew, jagged on broken hinges. The cicadas silent. Shadows. Behind rotted vines, through cracked panes, grey lace made white a moment in the failing sun of the still evening. The porch rail juts in disarray, splayed like finger bones. The yard is an expanse of hard baked earth. The grass dried to yellow. A little green showing through. Coarse, bristling nettles. It glistens below the sycamore tree. There is something red on the lawn.

Hollows like eyes. In the ash, the grey, the burnt lace, the glitter. Dark turns. Ashes drift, hesitant, a cold exhalation from the maw of broke, scorched, tumbledown boards. A cloud encroaches. Glass scattered, aglitter, stars on night's shore. Dust white in the gloom on wrenched stairs. The doors askew, jagged on broken hinges. The cicadas silent. Shadows. Behind rotted vines, through cracked panes, grey lace made white a moment in the failing sun of the still evening. The porch rail juts in disarray, splayed like finger bones. The yard is an expanse of hard baked earth. The grass dried to yellow. A little green showing through. Coarse, bristling nettles. It glistens below the sycamore tree. There is something red on the lawn.

Your breath catches. Hollows like eyes. In the ash, the grey, the burnt lace, the glitter. Dark turns. Ashes drift, hesitant, a cold exhalation from the maw of broke, scorched, tumbledown boards. A cloud encroaches. Glass scattered, aglitter, stars on night's shore. Dust white in the gloom on wrenched stairs. The doors askew, jagged on broken hinges. The cicadas silent. Shadows. Behind rotted vines, through cracked panes, grey lace made white a moment in the failing sun of the still evening. The porch rail juts in disarray, splayed like finger bones. The yard is an expanse of hard baked earth. The grass dried to yellow. A little green showing through. Coarse, bristling nettles. It glistens below the sycamore tree. There is something red on the lawn.

Blood leaks out. Your breathe catches. Hollows like eyes. In the ash, the grey, the burnt lace, the glitter. Dark turns. Ashes drift, hesitant, a cold exhalation from the maw of broke, scorched, tumbledown boards. A cloud encroaches. Glass scattered, aglitter, stars on night's shore. Dust white in the gloom on wrenched stairs. The doors askew, jagged on broken hinges. The cicadas silent. Shadows. Behind rotted vines, through cracked panes, grey lace made white a moment in the failing sun of the still evening. The porch rail juts in disarray, splayed like finger bones. The yard is an expanse of hard baked earth. The grass dried to yellow. A little green showing through. Coarse, bristling nettles. It glistens below the sycamore tree. There is something red on the lawn.

From the dark, over burnt and broken wood, parched soil, dead leaves, ugly nettles, a cold grasp like wet cloth. Blood leaks out. Your breathe catches. Hollows like eyes. In the ash, the grey, the burnt lace, the glitter. Dark turns. Ashes drift, hesitant, a cold exhalation from the maw of broke, scorched, tumbledown boards. A cloud encroaches. Glass scattered, aglitter, stars on night's shore. Dust white in the gloom on wrenched stairs. The doors askew, jagged on broken hinges. The cicadas silent. Shadows. Behind rotted vines, through cracked panes, grey lace made white a moment in the failing sun of the still evening. The porch rail juts in disarray, splayed like finger bones. The yard is an expanse of hard baked earth. The grass dried to yellow. A little green showing through. Coarse, bristling nettles. It glistens below the sycamore tree. There is something red on the lawn.

Black blood oozes into cracked soil. From the dark, over burnt and broken wood, parched soil, dead leaves, ugly nettles, a cold grasp like wet cloth. Blood leaks out. Your breathe catches. Hollows like eyes. In the ash, the grey, the burnt lace, the glitter. Dark turns. Ashes drift, hesitant, a cold exhalation from the maw of broke, scorched, tumbledown boards. A cloud encroaches. Glass scattered, aglitter, stars on night's shore. Dust white in the gloom on wrenched stairs. The doors askew, jagged on broken hinges. The cicadas silent. Shadows. Behind rotted vines, through cracked panes, grey lace made white a moment in the failing sun of the still evening. The porch rail juts in disarray, splayed like finger bones. The yard is an expanse of hard baked earth. The grass dried to yellow. A little green showing through. Coarse, bristling nettles. It glistens below the sycamore tree. There is something red on the lawn.

There is something red on the lawn. Black blood oozes into cracked soil. From the dark, over burnt and broken wood, parched soil, dead leaves, ugly nettles, a cold grasp like wet cloth. Blood leaks out. Your breathe catches. Hollows like eyes. In the ash, the grey, the burnt lace, the glitter. Dark turns. Ashes drift, hesitant, a cold exhalation from the maw of broke, scorched, tumbledown boards. A cloud encroaches. Glass scattered, aglitter, stars on night's shore. Dust white in the gloom on wrenched stairs. The doors askew, jagged on broken hinges. The cicadas silent. Shadows. Behind rotted vines, through cracked panes, grey lace made white a moment in the failing sun of the still evening. The porch rail juts in disarray, splayed like finger bones. The yard is an expanse of hard baked earth. The grass dried to yellow. A little green showing through. Coarse, bristling nettles. It glistens below the sycamore tree. There is something red on the lawn.

There is something in the fabric of old, silent places. Time seems to lay a patina on them, made of moss and lichen, of slow growing things, decay, stains and stillness. The stone, the wood, the earth, even the air holds something more than beauty. An immeasurable presence, a union of time past with the slowly burgeoning moment.

In summer here the long shadows of grass-blanketed barrows turn away the days, measuring aeons. Beyond the bare clearings, the hallowed arches and looming ranks of tangled evergreens confuse the way. Above the broken sky glows blue or shimmers black, growing to an intensity that swells those sheltered spaces. On those old mounds, on those grey stones, over those brooding trees, there is a softening as of erosion, the light gentle. Even summer storms traverse the patchwork fields and forests and sun dappled valleys in vast stately swathes.

As the days shorten, as the cold bites, as the sun becomes bone through the mist and mottled shroud, as fluid night flows through hearth, hollow and the empty places like a tide, you can sense something timeless stirring in the heart chambers of those cold earthen tombs. Shadows turn and lengthen. Moon dark creeps about them in the long watches of the night; what time they now measure seems beyond measuring. What thing is it, time turns about? In the distance, amid the wood, as the shadow lights upon a great jagged stone, a gleam of fire, now orange, now blue, in the night.

That erosion has wearied the fabric between the hollow, hungry morning of the world, and the somnolent now. What is it that wakes?

There has been a ghost story about the girl who died in the asylum, and was buried here, in the Dunbarrow Cemetery, beyond living memory. My father told me about it, his father told him. The local legend has been a right of passage for teenagers at least since the 50s. They'd drink some beers or smoke some weed and bike or drive up the long forest road at sunset, torches and headlights flickering, and scare each other with shouts, shadows and the story of Sad Susan, and scream at a cat's glowing eyes amongst the dried weeds, the crooked stones, the cold imploring statues.

Though that's not quite true. Time has made a game of the story, like whispers in the dark. Meaning layered like sands that become stone, currents eddying this way and that, sediments coloured by different stains, and except when a violent fault breaks the world open, only the surface shows.

On nights when storm surge battered the sea cliffs, torrents obscured the wider world and winds like tearing hands bent trees and ripped cables like threads, in a room lit orange by the light of kerosene lamps, father would tell the tale.

"Sad Susan they called her. Long dank hair, pale and thin and miserable and bony, but really just a slip of a thing, just a little older than you. They say she was in there, in the old Dunbarrow madhouse, because she cut up all her dollies. Or it might have been cats. The gullible say she scalpelled the nurse, stuck all sorts of paraphernalia in the holes…"

"What's paraphernalia?"

"Bits and pieces, bibs and bobs, what ever was lying to hand. Medical scissors and cotton bandages and false eyeballs and the like. It was their electric shock room and their eye doctoring room, go figure. They say she scalpelled and stuffed the nurse, got out of the electrode room, shocked into madness and screaming like a harridan, burnt the locked children's ward to ash, before leaping aflame from the tower, electricity dripping from her fingers. Everyone else in the old madhouse, the other nurses and doctors and patients in the unburnt buildings, were all found like this," and he'd thrust his face forward from shadow into the flickering orange light, eyes wide, red tongue protruding, *"krrrrrk*, all dead."

The same story, the same words, the same shrieks of delight and denial. Stories and shadow puppets before yellow flames, and we would laugh off the night's fears in the face of a ridiculous rictus.

Then in a lull after the laughter, even the storm quiet for a moment, the last line of the tale.

"You can see her unmarked stone glowing with fire and lightning in the last moment of the evening. Don't look too long, she might look back." Something in that challenge brought silence, the air chill, the lamplight weak, more shadow than illumination.

Grandfather would tell the tale with homemade lemonade and hard store biscuits on his porch in the waning afternoon, after an endless day of hide-and-seek, calling Sad Susan seeking, scaredy cats reeking! on the edge of the forest. As the day darkened someone, Danny Forrest or Tiff Mayweather or one of the other neighbourhood children would always end up weeping, calling, thinking they were lost. Sick of being it, or being sought, the game would change to one of war, with waved sticks and thrown pinecones. Of a sudden nobody wanted to be Sad Susan, no one wanted to be found by Sad Susan. War, it seemed, raucous shouts and scrapes and bruises kept thoughts of a gangling figure perhaps glimpsed stalking amongst the trees at bay.

In the safety of the porch, Grandfather would dismiss father's version as poppycock.

"I'll tell you about Sad Susan. Yes, when your father was a boy that big mansion up by the old cemetery was a mental institution, but it was modern and even had a pleasant sounding name: Summerfair Hospital. Nothing bad ever happened there, well, nothing out of the ordinary, until it filled with gas and burnt to a cinder. And those that didn't burn were asphyxiated, they choked on the gas. But that was an accident, not anything peculiar."

He'd always stop on peculiar, allow it to sink in, sip tea, offer biscuits, which we refused impatiently, because the next part of the tale was queer indeed.

"Before that," he continued, "it was The Our Lady Of The Angels Convent School, where nuns prayed the Angelus three times a day. That's a prayer that honours the moment the Angel of The Lord spoke to Mary, and she swelled with the Holy Spirit, that became Jesus H Christ if you pardon my French. Behold the handmaiden of the Lord, they'd sing, Be it done unto me according to Thy word. Now it was also a school that taught the Catholic girls hereabouts. This was back before the place was a hospital, before the war, and Sad Susan was just a slip of a girl. A pretty little thing —the aunt of a friend knew her.

"I suppose all that praying and bending got to some of those girls. Some girls just have a powerful urge to be wicked. That's the best and worst kind, if you take my meaning, so you lads steer clear of that sort. Puts me in mind of your grandmother, bless her heart, but that's another tale. Susan was clever and petulant and wicked, and she got caught flitting off the grounds at midnight to meet her beau.

"Now the Mother there was strict as nails, holy as a starched sheet, she declared the girl was off to meet Satan, thrashed her soundly, and locked her in the tower for the night. Which is what they did with penitents, and many a girl better behaved for it. But not Susan, no. She stamped her foot, she smashed the great round window with her hand, she cursed a blue streak and she threw her lamp down in a fit. It smashed on the flagstones at the foot of the tower and flames spread through the dry stalks of clinging ivy and licked up the walls.

"The good Mother had had the whole place bolted, locked and shuttered to forestall further escapades. Did Susan cry a warning? No, she sat there sad and petulant, and when the flames caught up the tower she threw herself down and broke on the stones.

"They say she caught fire anyway, and crawled away, and she was all sort of torn out of shape by the heat, and they found her near the big stone gate in the dawn when the fire marshall arrived, and she was the only one who got out.

"Now the gullible will tell you her unmarked stone in the old cemetery glows with the fires of hell in the twilight, where she still burns, but the practical will tell you that's just a particular quartz-stone they used for the marker, catching the light, just so."

Then with the last golden light of day a broken flicker through the trees, the crickets would hush for a moment, and we'd wonder why in our earlier games of stealth and silence, when everyone else was caught and answered the quiet call, there seemed to be someone who didn't.

Grandfather's Sad Susan was all the more frightening, told on a summer's evening, and we'd pile inside, flick on all the lights, and turn the TV on, loud. Just a few years later, with all the assured certitude of teens, dumb kids we'd think. Me, Danny, Terry and Charlie Markham. What dumb kids. But we'd still go up there, to see the stone in the last gleam of twilight.

Wisdom, of course, comes with a little patience, experience, hard lessons. Even a cursory examination of local folklore, yellowing newspapers, obscure biographies, parish records, reveals tale after tale. When Summerfair was the mansion of a late Victorian coal magnate, the tower the only visible remnant of a monastic bell tower, the new wing an airy thing of elegant cut sandstone, finely mortared, and tall deceptive windows, frilled with cast iron that only became bars and spikes upon a more diligent inspection, Sad Susan was a maid servant, in love with the scion of the family, lost at sea. Punished by the Lord, she burned the place, then hung from the gate, below the incised motto in the stone arch; Summer Fair, Winter Warn, just as her beloved returned to see her grim handiwork and the last light in her eyes. Her pauper's grave a blank white stone.

One hundred years earlier, a gothic anecdote in a parson's diary. A gypsy girl. Love, pain, fire fall, stone. In the time of King Charles, a holy novice, sin, impenitence, fire, immolation, cast from a cliff.

Earlier still, before any stones were laid, a village legend, a forest witch, love, pain, fire, fall, stone. Love, pain, fire, fall, stone. Love, pain, fire, fall, stone. And after, in the half-light, a figure in the forest.

An archeology of meaning; if one could sift tales like sand to find a flintsherd of truth, and decipher beyond the sweet illusion, what might one see? When tremulous life first fended off the fanged dark with raised arms and upraised voices, when the world was young and creatures barely human scrawled totems of their dreams and terrors in ochre and charcoal in subterranean stone galleries, crawling through the close confines to bury deep the things that preyed like flame and bone behind their skulls in the yearning gleam of the long starry dark. Perhaps, perhaps, if they could hide that thing in the utter dark it would no longer emerge at the dying of the day.

There are such pictures, found recently in caves like vast cracks in the sea cliffs, past grinding rocks, crevices dwindling to the deeper dark, unperturbed for millennia upon millennia, Incised marks, stained red and black, a stick figure? Not quite a man. A few sharp lines, indecipherable.

Like whispers in the dark, the illusion, the tale, the creature has taken on layers of meaning, layers of complexity. Guises for each moment, each age. Its most recent iteration, almost comical.

"They say she emerges from the barrow in the grounds. They say inside are the bones of some ancient, unknown people, entwined in strange ways, broken and worn away."

"You're good at this, Charlie, but I still want to know exactly who the hell are *they*?"

Charlie Markham was a skinny wretch with a mop of dark hair in front of dark eyes that always smirked. There was something he called a moustache above his top lip. There was a turn to his grin that people who didn't know him thought was insolence, though it was more like shyness hiding a ready wit. He sat on the hood of Danny's truck, smirking and sipping beer from a can. He had all the bravado and fragility of being fourteen.

"They. *They* is everyone. *They* is the collective subconscious. It's like *them* but bigger, more alien, more distant, more cold."

Danny was in the truck, dialling bursts of static on the radio, he finally got a station, an old song

— I just want another little piece of your heart babeee.

"I thought the collected unconscious was your dad and his pals after four bottles of cheap bourbon."

"Oh ha ha. You know when you talk to Millicent and her friends at school? That look on their faces is the collective unconscious."

"Oh ho."

"—that's what she said. Anyway, they say *she* was an angelic novice, a junior teacher, back when it was a Catholic school. That she was seduced by the convent's priest confessor, but when he got down to it, there were horns on her labia. He said the devil made him do it, and he did it with her anyway. Afterwards, he said she was an abomination and locked her in the tower room to pray. Instead she set herself on fire and jumped from the window."

"If she was your girlfriend you wouldn't care if she had horns on her labia," yelled Danny.

"I wouldn't care if she had horns on her head," retorted Charlie.

"You'd do her even if she had fangs."

"You'd do her even if she had fangs and horns."

"You'd do her even if she had fangs and horns and a beard."

"Dude, I'd especially do her if she had fangs and horns and a beard."

"You wouldn't know what to do with her."

"Would too."

"Man, she'd eat you up and spit you out. And break your bones."

"She must be on the voluptuous side."

"Like Millicent."

"Just because you like them stick thin and black hearted."

"Hey, Milo, what are labia?"

"Dudes, you guys are funny, but what about respecting the dead. She's buried here. Just over there. I'm sure she was a kind, sad girl," I said laughing.

"Milo, pass a beer. It's just a story. That mound in the yard isn't even a barrow. It's a fallout shelter built in the 1950s."

"There's still barrows, in the deeper woods. Hey, look, it's glowing."

Catching the last of the evening light, amid the grey and weathered stones and statues, the long shadows of the trees, the low white block like an empty marble plinth unevenly sunk into the soft earth stood bright, as if caught under sudden moonlight. There was no moon.

"Wow, have you put you headlights on?" I asked Danny.

"No, no I haven't. that's amazing."

"It's just a trick of the light," said Charlie.

"What's that?"

"It's just a cat."

"It's standing up."

My father's story, my grandfather's story, the old stories and the new, they all agreed that the stone glowed. Everything else was a jumble of whispers and lurid grins. Nothing consistent, nothing that even hinted at truth.

Of course, that didn't explain the wracked, skeletal thing the colour of ashes and earth with black holes for eyes in a broke-faced skull now staggering toward us, the decayed tatters of the shift it wore, clinging to leathern sinew, dripping filth, still showing traceries of delicate embroidery.

"Oh shit," said Danny. "This is the shit. Did you set this up?" Danny was a practical guy. Big boned, blonde, square jawed. A footballer, a mechanic. In another moment his solid jaw quaked. His eyes shadowed, his brow collapsed in a disbelieving frown. Then he visibly blanched. It was closer, under the trees now. I could see a centipede writhing in its filthy hair, the rays of the sun visible through rents in the fabric of the thing's chest.

Charlie crawled from the hood in through the truck's open window, without his feet touching the ground.

A moment later, the thing moved. Flying toward us in a sweep both swift and ungainly, like a great, brittle mantis. By that time the tyres were spitting dust, Danny and Charlie were gone. And I, the fearful, the gullible, chilled and tingling from mere stories, stood with the grim spirit, the revenant, the horror, an arms length before me, heart slowed and massively thumping, rigid as it reached broken, blackened fingers toward me.

Its claws touched my chest. My heart stopped. An exhalation, cold, cold, earthen and cold, froze sweat on my brow, tainted my lips. It inched closer, like a reluctant lover approaching a tentative kiss. I could feel heat spilling from my body in waves. I could feel it, it quickening, as the heat drained from me.

Through rattling teeth I could barely utter, "I love you, Susan. I love you."

In the stillness it stopped. My heart thumped to life again. Its head seemed to tilt to a quizzical angle, as if to say, *"My love? I've been waiting for you."*

She took my hand in a shy, uncompromising claw, and we staggered toward the distant, derelict building, all scorched bone grey walls and broken black beams behind high, chain link fencing and tangled bracken. Pines shadowing cathedral-like the crumbling road to the asylum gate, a high arch surmounted by chimeric gargoyles, a weathered inscription in old, old stones, now indecipherable in the bruised twilight.

Through the arch, in the semi-dark, I glimpsed flame flicker and shadow dancing.

Time seemed to slow, each step interminable, measured to a single heartbeat seeming loud like a muffled bell hammered to the point of breaking.

We staggered on, the she-thing sometimes pointing to the gate, hollow sockets somehow fixing me with enquiry, the shadow fire beyond it a realm of torment I knew from whence there was no return. I could hear it under the dry, soughing pines, not a sound but a writhing in the ears, like maggots, and amid the tintinnabulation a vibration, a hum, swelling to a roar. And Danny s F100 pick-up skidded to a halt beside me, spraying gouts of dank soft earth, filling the air with mouldering pine, the same old song still blaring out the radio,

Another little piece of your heart babeeeeee...

"What was it? Where's it gone? we came back for you, Milo, get in the car." Charlie was shivering in the passenger seat, bent over retching. Danny was craning out the window, seeing right through her.

She turned, her attention fixed on him with a hunger. Then he saw. She grabbed his face in one swift lunge, sinew like iron on jagged bone, and pulled him bodily, half out of the car. With a gnarled black finger she hooked out his eye in a spurt of blood and fluids. She took the squashed thing and pressed it into her socket, where it oozed like a white, limpid slug.

Charlie leapt from the car, stumbling. She was on him like some grizzled mantis, pelvis like a bear trap from which protruded horns, black and curved like spider fangs, ridged like rams horns, dripping something like venom, pinning him to the road.

His limbs juddered, leaving a silhouette like a snow angel in the carpet of pine needles, and he screamed and screamed, until she had his tongue out, still spawning in her fingers, while he gurgled and drowned in blood. She opened her black toothed jaw and placed the ragged red thing inside, and sat straddling Charlie, until he was still.

In that moment I bent and picked up a hard, round lump of rock, as big as a fist, the same dull black stone shot through with grey as many of the grave markers. In that moment I thought to smash her head, to smash my own. But she turned, and spoke, a voice little more than a rasping breath, or the scraping of boughs.

"My love," she said. *"Come."*
She rose, and I followed.

We stood before the gate, shadow fires flickering beyond, and Sad Susan said again, *"My Love,"* and clutched me in her bone embrace.

I took the stone, grasped so tight the grit scored my fingers, and thrust it up, under her spidering black rib cage, through leathern flesh and the desiccated remnants of what had been inside her, and lodged it where she had no heart.

Sad Susan kissed me, let go, and drifted through the gate.

The girl I loved had a heart of stone.

The papers called me 'Mad Milo', the authorities said I desecrated the grave and then the corpse of a long dead girl, and then when my friends tried to stop me, I battered and gutted them, Danny and Charlie, in some kind of drug addled rage. They have me jacketed and drugged and monitored and talked to in a facility a long way away.

Now in this place, all fluorescent light, grimed white walls an eternity of neither night nor day, I can't get the smell of something like anaesthetic, and something like burnt bones, out of my nose. My fingers are black and weary. Daubed scenes of torment alongside banal stick figures in muddy colours on ragged butcher's wrap paper the walls. I don't know which, for me hold more fear, which I am trying to exorcise, in the dark. Shadows and flames in my skull. I ache with finger painting.

Because of rationalisation, they are renovating *that* place. Like so many times before. Rebuilding, recommissioning. Reopening.

It will be state of the art. The happiest place on Earth. When they rationalise *this* place, we shall all be moving there. Where, I'm sure, Sad Susan, with her withered eye, her rank tongue, her sharp ragged bones and her stone cold heart is dancing with the fire shadows, waiting, waiting for me.

From this window the thing arches out over deep blue water, resting on stone pillars like fortifications. I could take picture after picture, but there is something despicable about the progress of the black iron beams, jutting like broken bones, the glowing rivets like Christ wounds, the figures crawling over it like maggots and flies and ants, rather than tearing down to its constituent molecules, spewing up piecemeal the swollen carcass of leviathan.

The two halves of the thing grow closer each day. From this oblique angle, on the second floor of the offices of Empire Art & Photography, it is not so much an arch but a complex and impossible prison, all harsh and tortured angles. There's something unholy about it. The rampart of hell. I've seen men fall, so far, to an ocean seething grey and hard as glass.

"The wonder of the age, eh, Trev. There's not a bridge like it anywhere in the world." Morton Pewtress, proprietor of Empire Art & Photography, fans himself with the paper, rubs it against his sweating brow, where it leaves a stain of ink . There's a picture of the skeletal arch amongst the folds, and a few letters of a headline. The sea breeze brings the discordant campanology and shouts of construction, engines and cries, a constant distant tolling, but doesn't cool the room, much.

"Unholy," I mutter.

"Eh?" Says Morty.

"Hot." He suddenly slams the folded paper to the desk, crushing a fly. A big ugly brute, red eyed and glistening. There's a faint smell like burning and maybe like pus from the thing as I turn the paper over. Now a black and red smear across Births, Deaths & Marriages.

"Got him," Morty says, without much enthusiasm. His face is red and crumpled, creased and bristly. His eyes behind gleaming lenses bulbous. There is something insect-like about his balding head and scrawny, wrinkled neck.

"There's twins in Petersham, probably Catholic. One in Ultimo, one in Glebe, one in Annandale, one in Newtown. Well you know the score, big family, doubly blessed and all that. Start there and work your way back." He stood a moment, rolling back and forth on the balls of his feet, thumbs hooked through striped braces. A grin on his face like you'd think he wanted to eat them, not photograph them.

"Oh there's a summons in Balmain. Maybe there first."

"Can't you do that? You're better at it than I am. More convincing."

"Can't. I have an Ethel in the darkroom. Papers are on the desk." That jackal grin. He rolled on his heels and creaked back down stairs.

'Ethels' were young girls with stars in their eyes. Morty had them thinking they'd be the next Ethel Merman or Jessie Matthews, but after a short while for nothing more than a promise he'd have them posing in their skimpies. How he did it, a detestable old bug like Morton, I don't know. He had a convincing murmur, a slow hypnotic patter, allaying fears and painting dreams. Sometimes I suspected he plied them with barbitone in a tot of brandy. The fumes of photographic chemicals that wafted up from the studio below had a clean, cold smell. Sometimes there was something pungent, something sharper.

Some packages of photos he sold for a few bob. Some apparently commanded higher prices. A clientele of parliamentarians, judges, perverts and police, Morty would quip. I just did the baby portraits. And sometimes the summons.

I tore the front page off the paper and crumpled 'The Eighth Wonder' into a ball and scraped the fragments of insect into the waste paper basket. Pulled up a well thumbed telephone directory and set to work.

In red Morty's heavy hand had defaced the page, with gouged scribbles circling here and there blotchy black text, identifying likely prospects.

BIRTHS, MARRIAGES & DEATHS

Announcements under this heading shall be authenticated with the name and address of the sender, and are inserted in the "The Western Register," "Chronicle" and "Telgraph-Express" at a charge of Two Shillings Threepence when not exceeding five lines; over five lines Sixpence per line.

MILLWAITE *On the 3rd December, to Mrs Jonas Millwaite, of Angel St, Newtown, delivered of a SON,*

George Edward. Congratulations from your loving parents, and all the family.

HUNGERFORD. *On the 27th November, to Mrs Samule G Hungerford, of The Crescent, Annandale at St John's Maternity, delivered of TWINS, a son Pietyr William, a daughter, Alexandra-Jane, Doubly blessed. Congratulations are sent from Captain & Mrs William Hungerford of Portsmouth, England, Lt. George Hungerford of Calcuttta, Abigail…*

There was something appealing to me in the misspelling of old Samuel G Hungerford's name, and twins was always double your luck, so I found Hungerford, The Crescent, Annandale in the book, and dialled the exchange and subscriber number. It rang and rang, hollow and seemingly becoming more insistent, and I thought an operator would break in to tell me my party wasn't available, but then a voice, breathy and tentative spoke in the silence.

"Hello?"

I launched straight in, best not to give them time to think, "Congratulations on your new additions, Ma'am, you've been selected to receive free and complimentary a beautiful hand-tinted portrait of the new additions to your family, framed in your choice of gilt wood or the latest gilt plaster of Paris display. Our photographer will be calling today for your convenience at your home, so need even to come into the studio."

"I don't believe I asked for such a service, young man."

"Perhaps a relative then, let's see, we have a name here, a Lieutenant George Hungerford, perhaps? I'm sure the child's aunts and uncles, and indeed the grandparents will also want this heirloom service. I'm sure you don't want to disappoint."

"Oh, that seems unlikely."

"We'll be in your area this afternoon. Our photographer will call around midday."

"Young man, young man, I tell you …at peril. You don't…"

"Thank you Ma'am for your time." The key was to brook no refusal. In person, with the gleaming equipment, the selection of frames, the affable and highly skilled photographic artist trained in London and Paris, namely myself, the suckers rarely said no. We'd hard sell the French gilt frames, life-like colour process, Morton's special preservative treatment - your picture guaranteed not to fade for a hundred years!, and numerous duplicates, all at extra cost. All on the never never.

Collections was the hard part. The part I didn't like. Morton had a feel for it. There was something implacable about him. Like a python swallowing a puppy. After a couple of increasingly brusque letters of demand, threatening lawyers and courts and bailiffs, we'd turn up on the doorstep, official looking form in hand, claiming to be a sheriff's bailiff and if the cash wasn't forthcoming, with the legally constituted right to take possession of goods, jewellery, radio sets, any chattels to the value of. For a few sheets of photographic paper in some shabby cast painted plaster we'd take them for 30 or 40 quid. Well, Morton would. I just photographed babies. Mostly. Except today.

The official looking documents were in a black leather portfolio embossed with a gold coat of arms. Lions rampant facing across a shield bearing a ship and a castle. I think it was the menu holder from a hotel in Bristol. The documents themselves had more swirls and curlicues than a guinea note. Of course a real *Fieri Facias* was a plain looking printed document with some busy sounding Latin, unassuming official stamps and illegible signatures, their curliness in exact proportion to the self importance of the beak and the clerks who signed them. I should know, I'd seen a few. Morton had found there was something in the theatricality of the elaborate that convinced the punters.

Today's were June and Jack Mulready, of William Lane, Balmain East, who'd had 9 hand tinted, gilt arched portraits of their coal haired pride and joy — Valentine. Valentine! I ask you. Morty had photographed him, a dreadful little homunculus, he said, who managed to knock over one camera, and spent the rest of the time alternately pissing and crying. Watch the birdie wasn't cutting the mustard, so he had to surreptitiously pinch the little blighter on one fat ham hock, and captured the most angelic look of round-faced wonderment. The doting parents loved it, but still didn't pay the bill. Some £28,6s,8d.

Morton was giggling like a schoolgirl with some strumpet in white face and a shimmy dress. The lecherous old vampire. She was shaking her spangles and singing *Boop boop de doop* like a cartoon dolly bird. Portraits of the staid and prim and stern looked on from the walls, disapproval almost palpable.

I gathered up *The Kaiser*, a Deckrullo-Nettel press camera made in Germany just after the war. In gleaming teakwood, a red leather bellows, brass folding struts and hinges and a rotating arrangement of brass lenses on the front for portraits, landscapes and close-ups, it had a certain Imperial monocled military aspect —thus the nickname.

Some days here the sky and sea are a blue that you can only imagine is the blue of paradise, resonating each the other, the sea glimmer the silvering of her eyes, the sky bright as a fever dream. Not today. Today the sea is the lead colour of a drowning man's last breath, the sky the grey of asphyxia.

That is to say the heat is oppressive. The traffic on Broadway sent up a waving fume, and the inside of the black Bedford 8CWT van was choking, leaving a taste like meths and week old meat in the back of my throat.

Harris St the air cleared, and the traffic thinned, and I though about my spiel while I trundled down towards the Glebe Island Bridge, another monster of iron fret work, this one a platform pivoting open like some damnable playground see-saw gone askew, to allow ships to pass either side on the pitiless waters below. I avoided thinking about it, instead girded my approach.

Sometimes it was best to go in guns blazing, play the hard man. Others all solicitation and sympathy. Something about the heat and the bridges, the constriction of the wool jacket, the knot of the tie, made going the hard mug seem the thing to do. And something about the house. A ramshackle brick and sandstone terrace with sheets drying on the sagging rails of the second floor balcony, cracked glass panes reflecting the sluggish waters and crane gantries of the dockyards across the way.

At least the fence and gate were new. The wrought iron railings and stylised spear heads had a gleam to them, the blacked metal a coldness even in the heat. One half of the head high arch fell to the ground with a screech and a clatter as soon as I pushed on it.

A woman was coming through the door quick as you like, broom in one hand, gin bottle in an apron pocket.

"Here, that's new. My Jack won't like that. Not one little bit." She had a face like a wizened apple, rot brown and pushed in. I thought there was something touched or simple about her. As I stepped over the toppled gate, up to the door, I noticed it was her hands smelled of gin, not her breath.

"The gate doesn't appear to have the bolts in the hinges yet."

"Not finished yet."

That was plain. Polite but hard. Insistent. A hard sentiment to muster after a farcical beginning, I stepped up, brandishing my documents.

"Mrs Mulready, I have been authorised by the office of the Sheriff and the Bailiff to make demand of full payment for the outstanding debt you have incurred for monies owing to Empire Art and Photography for pictures of your son…"

"Not my son."

"…Valentine."

"Ah, now you see that's where you're mistaken." From the appearance of a gin soaked simp, with a lowering of her head and her voice, she seemed to take on a harder aspect, like someone who spent long hours wringing blood soaked cloths in leather hard hands.

"You see the hoers (she said it ho-ers), they come to me when they need fixing, when they've got one in the belly, and I get rid of it for 'em, but some can't pay because they like the gin or the hops or the horses a little too much, so we take the next one, and sell it on. There's lots of ladies and some gents that want a handsome babby, and willing to pay a good quid for it too. My lad's hoers cry a bit about it, so we give 'em one of those fancy pictures, and to the buyers too. The girls that cry too much, well they're in the bay, and that's where my Jack'll be leaving you."

Again the screech of metal, and turning from the woman's yellow ape grin, there was a narrow but wizened man, as like to the woman as a knotted stick to a torn stump, yet still and obviously the remnants of the same tree, with his white knuckle fists and two tone shoes perched high on the other half of the arched gate and riding it grinning too, crashing down on top of me.

I woke on wet oil filmed sand. The back of my suit and my hair wet through. A pain in my head like I'd been hit by an iron gate. Go figure. Though I could still sense the heat, there was a numbness to my arms, a lead heaviness to the fingers. The waters made a sucking sound, there was a smell of brine in my nostrils, and the sting of it in my eyes. The loading cranes above the wharfs teetered and menaced insect-like as I stood.

I staggered up to the van, still parked at the end of the ramshackle lane. Something had gone wrong in the Mulready's efforts to pitch me in the harbour with their dead whores and abortions, but we wouldn't be collecting any money today. Morty would take the loss out of my cut. I brushed myself off, a professional, *an artist*, Paris and London, by God and Hell and the deep blue sea. I'd photograph the Hungerford twins come burning bridges, hell or high water, so the day wouldn't be a total loss.

There is something about this part of town, the wide pleasant streets, the unassuming prosperity, a nut smell, a smell of eucalyptus, that even in a hard summer smells of distant seas and the close wet leaves of autumn. Cold valleys and quiet trees.

It was a relief, the sky had stopped its incessant beating. The Hungerford house was towering thing, with a hint of fairy tale and sea-faring about it. Mansard roofs , gables, towers either side, with porticoed balconies and porthole windows. Neat with delicate, freshly painted woodwork and gleaming, well dressed blue stones.

The door too was freshly painted, spotless. It was cool under the porch. I lifted *The Kaiser* from where he was resting on his tripod legs, and rang the ship's bell, hung from a bracket by the doors. There was a distant rustling. Quiet. A closer rustling.

The woman that answered the door was delicate, bird like, somehow worn smooth rather than weathered by age, she seemed poised, about to retreat or flee, if something should suddenly pique her alert and tremulous listening. There was an overpowering smell of flowers emanating from the dark behind her, and the funerary Victorian finery she wore, the white lace gone to grey, the black silk washed out like ink reeked of must and lavender.

With my free hand I tipped a hat that I wasn't wearing and launched straight into the spiel, "Trevallyn Peran, Ma'am, Trevor for short, representing Empire Art & Photography on behalf of the Telegraph and may I congratulate you on the recent, joyous addition to your family? By publishing your announcement in the paper you were entered into the draw to win a complimentary, heirloom quality portrait of your new darlings, for you and your family members to proudly display on your walls. Excuse me, ma'am, it's hot and this thing is heavy. May I step in? Thank you."

She assented with a nod, or perhaps she heard something? in the distant stillness, and retreated. I stepped past into the cool and closed the door.

"All that is required to receive the free portrait of your loved ones is to order an additional framed print for another family member. Both will be hand tinted and coloured, finished with our scientifical process, to preserve them for future generations, and framed in either traditional elegance or in a moderne Parisienne style. I believe our office confirmed arrangements with a Lieutenant Hungerford, and ..."

"That seems hardly likely."

Her lead-paint face was bright in the gloom. The hall was long and deep and dark, like a chasm or mineshaft, pillared with bulbous Chinese vases on turned wooden stands, overflowing with wilting, lilies and sprays of lavender. The distance was vertiginous. From high on the walls glowered dour portraits, bristling Victorians with bizarre whiskers and bright vests, peculiar in contrast, at the end hung a painted and sculptured Christ with a garish glow and bloody eyes, luminous in torture.

"These fellows seem a bit dusty, we could organise fresh, modern portraits of the whole family."

"You have sharp eyes young man."

"Thank you, Ma'am. Years of looking down a camera."

"I do not mean perspicacious or observant. I mean squinty, narrow. Narrow eyes give a man a shrewd or sinister look."

"Nothing shrewd or sinister about me, Ma'am."

The house reeked of old wealth and something sick, and of a sudden I was reeling.

"You look quite peaked, young man." She fixed me with the black and unfathomable eyes of a carrion bird.

"Thank you Ma'am, as a young man I had ergot poisoning. It left me wastrel. Perhaps the dark."

"The whole family, you say? Come." A secret smile cornered her lips, like that of an ingenue, a sweet sixteen who thought perhaps of a kiss stolen from her shy and innocent beau.

"We have had fever in the home recently. Gone now, of course. All gone. Something out of the sub-continent —unknown to science. We have the dubious honour of having now entered into the annals of discovery —*Hungerford Fever.*"

We strolled the corridor, like gentlefolk taking a turn, lost in musing, and stopped by a door that she silently opened.

"Here is father, recently back from Malaya on a packet. He was a Captain and trader for many years. Saw many changes. Sail to steam to diesel. Now he sails other shores."

Her hand gripped my wrist. I expected a claw, but it was gentle, almost coaxing. That smile again. I could not turn away. In the room on a trestle, fringed with a heavy black valence, was coffin, huge.

He was a handsome, brawny man, in younger days, as a portrait of a uniformed sailor on the wall behind the vessel attested. The box was a rich red teak, polished to a high shine, with hempen rope handles. Candles flickered as she steered me away.

"Come, come."

At the next door, three similar coffins. Slighter. Arrayed in a row. Ship shape and with portraits of young men, with broad pleasant smiles, thick hair and square cheeks. All similar, all a little different. Serious but calm, open eyes.

"Here are the boys. My brothers. Sailors to a man. Their eyes filled with depths and horizons, and cheer. They would come home with such cheer. Such cheer. Like an evening zephyr after a stultifying calm. Here now."

"Here now, Henry and Caleb's wives, who became my sisters. See how beautiful they are? Though yes, these portraits are some years old. Young Joseph was still wild and fancy free."

This room was flowers, flowers, flowers, the boxes ornate. Ebonized wood stepped like ziggurats and with angular handles and corners in polished brass. The portraits showed stately young women, with demure smiles, in gowns quite flowing and medieval, and surrounded by foliage, perhaps styled after the seasons.

"Finally. Here are Henry's angels. The twins. So young. Step in. Step closer."

She closed the door, with a dull thump that echoed out the still hall, the fading rooms.

"The coffin maker isn't finished yet.. So weak and frail, yet almost the last to die. I am expecting delivery today. So they lie in their crib, still. There are no portraits of them. You will take one."

They lay under embroidered satin, laid out in a parody of rest, hands in prayer on the white covers, two babies too young ever to have uttered a prayer to the Lord. Faces in a grinning rictus, skin blue grey and yellow mottled, like old bruises. Between them a red candle in a glass tulip on an ebonized holder, guttering, so a shadow moved across the faces. Wisps of hair on the tight skulls seemed to sough as under a gentling hand.

"So they can join us."

Now her hand *was* like a claw. I set up *The Kaiser* one handed, spilling magnesium powder in the flash, unable to shake her relentless grip. I angled its gleaming eyes over the small and indistinct features, their weak downturned mouths, in the shadow flicker, a movement like mewling. The candle between them would leave a burning whiteness on the plate, a heat, perhaps signifying a presence that I could not determine if grace or damnation.

I lifted the candle holder and a black ichor oozed from the felt underneath; cold and thick like syrup it wet my hand and a stench like liquor and brine and rank marshes stung my nostrils. Through watering eyes I could see tendrils of the stuff on the sheets,

"Gah!" I dropped the thing and it broke and guttered, and flamed. I wiped the ooze from my fingers on a kerchief, and tossed it on the floor. The flames licked up redly, but still she would not loose her grip. I flailed for the cord, the switch that opened the shutter.

In the flash the grip released. I saw the smiles, and grabbing the camera, ran

Outside the world gleamed like silver nitrate on wet paper, the world made monochrome by searing fire bleaching all colour, the luminous blue above speaking of garish hand tinting, sheer white made cold and black blushed giving a semblance of puppet life. Printed and painted. Those going about their day, in the street, in their cars, rushing to see the flames, yet in oblivion, oblivious.

Outside the offices of Empire Art & Photography, a great insect lay crumpled, white, bloated in the gutter, on the hot black asphalt, under the wheels of police wagon, in its head eyeless caverns glittering with broken glass.

Men in uniforms lifted floorboards with crowbars and spades. In the cavity unnderneath limbs and torsos in gleaming monochrome, faces hand tinted, in glorious diorama scientifically preserved with the fluids of his special process, lay all of Morton's dolly birds, hollow eyed as he.

My eyes ache but men look through me. One seems to speak but I neither hear nor listen; perhaps I am mistaken. Time passes in magnesium flashes, and at last there is stillness.

Except for the sky. Except for the bridge.

On a day like this, storm wracked, the bridge extends into a billowing abyss, its great fortifications no defence against that other realm, now visible. In the churning mist, on its dull steel pinions, figures grey-blue, mottled and wizened crawl, smiling, halt, beckoning.

I think I am the only man with tasks incomplete today on this behemoth's bony carcass.

Soon I will go.

The gunshots cracked all day.

The gunshots cracked all day, from when the sun blazed into the blue above the eastern pasture, beyond the rusting frame of the old windmill, the sentinel tower by the rust-barnacled water-tank that had been the fortress of so many childhood imaginings, to when it fell, casting a thickening bloody light over the wheat field, west of the house and barn, whose upward grade made it seem a vast expanse extending to the horizon.

The ripeness of that wheat, that ugly stunted rust-ridden wheat, and its seeming immensity under that sanguinary sun, were lies. Hollow betrayals of light and land.

The gunshots woke me. A distant, dry cracking. As dry as the hot wind rushing the fields of dead brittle wheat.

I pulled on my jeans and boots and ran through the kitchen, grabbing a piece of as yet unbuttered toast from Margaret's hand as I passed, before she had time to slather on the rich yellow stuff. She stood holding the butter knife. Her face, that despite her tremendous appetite, had of late been losing its cherubic aspect, formed its stern motherly look, her eyebrows rising.

"Grandad said not to...he'll be livid!" But I had kicked open the screen door and was running for what I thought would be the last time to my tower.

I clambered up the iron frame, as high as the just risen sun, and sat on the wooden platform below the rust eaten triangles of the blades. I could see Grandad, a small figure in white beside the carnival red tractor. The dust-red Hereford herd, their white faces skulls, milling before him. Grandad pushed up his hat and dabbed at his brow with a red bandanna. Then he tied it around the barrel of the .33 Winchester, slung with a strap over his shoulder, and taking bullets from a box on the nose of the tractor began thumbing them into the breech.

I watched, shocked to the guts, yet fascinated, as he lifted the butt to his shoulder, and taking careful aim pumped bullets into the heads of the curiously calm and lowing cattle.

A red star exploded on the white skulls. The cows would loose their dung and drop suddenly, and I could imagine their eyes rolling with surprise and momentary pain, as they staggered and fell heavily to their sides raising a burst of dust. Some, their legs would kick a little, searching for the hard earth, before they were finally still.

Occasionally a beast would meander away from the herd, then Grandad would whistle a particular whistle, and Petersen, our black and white Collie cattle dog, with lip's pulled back in a fool's grin that when he snarled became a sneer, would leap around and bark and nip at their ankles until the straying beast had returned to the herd.

When a dozen or so were dead Grandad would climb into the tractor, kick over the engine with a spurt of diesel exhaust, and then reversing, using the grader on the back, push the carcasses into a ditch.

From my tower I watched Grandad's methodical labour. When half the herd lay dusty in the ditch, when the sun was a rage of gold high in the immense and oppressive blue, and the shadows of the windmill were little more than the lines of some curious hexagram scored in the earth directly below, so that my tower seemed of a sudden not so high as it had always previously been, I returned to the house.

Grandad came in with the purpling dusk. From the front room, amongst the suitcases and packed cardboard cartons, Margaret and I heard his boots clump heavily up the steps. We turned from the television murmuring quietly before us to watch him through the screen door.

Sweat ran down his arm from the rolled sleeve of his shirt, trickled over his fingers and steamed off the barrel of the Winchester, a blue mist under the bare globe that lit the porch, just a shade lighter than the gunmetal itself. He made a circling motion with the rifle, so that the bow of the kerchief tied around the end of the barrel licked the dust off the floorboards. Then he dropped it. A shot rang out the evening, with a certain finality, and Margaret clutched Zebediah, her toy horse, tighter in her hands.

Grandad's eyes in his weathered face, as dark and wizened as a dried apple, were rolling then staring, bloodshot and mad and had he not been such a hard man they probably would have been tear filled. He seemed not to have heard or noticed the shot at all. Eyes rolling and staring into the blackening night, as mad as Old Bent Back's, Margaret's pony, the day he'd eaten jimson weed and gone wild.

We'd had to shoot Old Bent Back. It looked like we'd have to shoot Grandad too. Margaret would cry but she always did. She cried for a week when we shot Old Bent Back, until Grandad had made with wire and straw and glue and some of Old Bent Back's mane, a small bedraggled unicorn, with a horn he'd carved from a steer's cropped horn. Old Bent Back's soul was in that unicorn, Margaret said. She named it Zebediah and that had quietened her.

There were speckles of blood dried to black on Grandad's shirt and on his moleskins. Moths and gnats and mosquitos and iridescent beetles flickered around his head. He chucked off his hat, brushing at the insects which swarmed again around his ash-grey hair. He stomped through the front room without barely a nod at Margaret and I, and went down the hall to shower.

He was mad yesterday. Today he was crazy.

It wasn't the drought that had ruined our earth, like it had so many others. Grandad was canny. He'd used the last overdraft to stock up on cattle feed. Said he could smell a dry season coming on the breeze from the west. The government had deregulated the market, though. Imported beef from Asia was cheaper than our dust. It cost more to truck the herd to auction than what we'd get for it. South West Queensland Beef and Dairy owned the trucking. They owned the auction yards. They owned the abattoir, the estate agent and the bank. We were shafted.

The bank delivered the foreclosure notice and posted the auction signs. A South West Queensland Beef and Dairy subsidiary would buy our farm, our cattle, like they had so many others, and razor a profit while we yet owed them our labour and our blood.

Grandad wouldn't even let the suit from the real estate borrow a shovel to dig the post holes. Perfectly within his rights, Sheriff Flynn said. The bastard had to drive the 127 kilometres back to Windorah to get a shovel.

Soon as the Sheriff and the bankers and the estate agents had gone Grandad took a can of petrol and doused the *Auction: Foreclosure* signs and set them blazing.

"Bastards. Sweating collared men," he spoke with derision, "with narrow eyes and small minds. The suits that hang on their crooked shoulders like the hunched wings of carrion birds. Vultures, let them profit and feast on carcasses." He didn't curse much, especially in front of Margaret, so when he did you knew he meant it.

Margaret just said how pretty the flames looked, all halloween orange, burning triangles within squares livid against the dusk.

Me, I said nothing. I knew it was futile. I just could smell the burning in the air. It seemed to herald...something special, like Christmas Eve and the last day of school and the day after the finish of harvest all together. An expectancy of something new, change and freedom yet also an ending. Everything complete, but not quite, and everything about to start again but not quite yet.

After dinner of greens and carrots and lamb roast that Margaret had put on in the afternoon, a dinner at which no one said as much as 'Pass the salt please', Grandad sat on his wicker chair on the porch drinking straight from a bottle of Johnny Walker he'd been keeping for a celebration. He'd given that bottle to Dad ten years ago when Margie was born. Mum and Dad had died only a month later in a car smash.

I was four then, so although I remembered a lot about them, the smell of Mum's perfume and Dad's rough chin, and the sound of both their voices, Grandad had always been there too. That bottle had sat dusty and incelebrate on the shelf ever since. Yeah, tonight Grandad was celebrating.

We did the washing up and Margaret helped me with my algebra homework; she was good at that sort of thing, I never had the patience. Then we watched TV for a while, a program set in the lush English countryside. I couldn't bear it, the taste of dust still dry on my tongue, so went to bed.

But the moon lifted huge and butter-yellow over the fields out my window, and I was too restless to sleep. There was a smell, heady on the warm breeze, like when we'd drive into Windorah along the highway, past the abattoir.

As I turned my mind to what the city'd be like (we'd be going in just under a month, after the auction, to stay with Aunt May in Brisbane) and began finally drifting into dreams, I heard Grandad go out into the night, the creak of the barn door, and then, like the breaking of clock whose mechanism yet refused to fail completely, the rustle and twang of bailing wire, extolling some purely imaginary hour.

Margaret woke me earlier than the sun and said she couldn't find Grandad. She'd cooked a big breakfast of sausage and egg and fried tomato, and had made both tea and coffee. Because she knew Grandad was a bit sad because he'd had to shoot all the cattle and even his horses to stop the bankers taking them, but when she went to wake him he wasn't there. He'd even let the chickens out, and Petersen had killed a whole mess of them and was chasing the rest around.

"And I'm absolutely livid!" she added, (she'd heard the word 'livid' on TV and had been applying it liberally ever since) pointing at the breakfast, now cooling, laid on the best Gingham cloth, with Zebediah clutched in her hand. Her cheeks were flushed as she held her face tight against the welling tears.

I went and looked. There were feathers and bloody chicken carcasses scattered around the yard. The rooster, escaped into the lower branches of a scraggly gum by the coop, whose wire door hung only by the lower hinge, crowed mournfully.

Petersen was barking and chasing a chicken that he'd half mauled so it was running with its torn off head, held by one or two gory tendons, dragging a trail in the dust. The dog was well on its way to becoming wild. There was blood on his white bib, and he gave me barely a glance as I shouted his name, and that more snarling-guilty than cowed, before seizing the chicken and setting down to jaw it.

Then under the crystalline blue of the shadowless pre-dawn, a blue that of a sudden raged as the rim of the sun flared on the horizon, we saw something glinting, moving in the wheat field. Margaret, standing by me on the porch pointed with Zebediah clutched in her hand, its horn piercing.

The glinting, silver and gold and shimmering as the sun licked it, made a twangy chimey music as it dashed amongst the wheat. Silver fire aspark amid the sombre ochre of the field, it raised a dust haze as it ran, kicking the earth and crushing the heads to powder. It swung something into the air, a crook'd stick, a scythe that caught the sun and arc on its blade against the cerule morning.

It was Grandad. I could see tufts of his ashen hair through the wire cap on his head. He'd wrapped himself in bailing wire and was hacking at the wheat with the scythe like some madly animate scarecrow. He'd leap and twang and chime and slash a might slash out of the dead dry wheat. In the gusts of powder, he looked like some emaciated Michelin Man, like the one on the paint peeling sign at Murray's Tyre and Gas in Windorah.

He seemed to weary. I wasn't sure if he'd noticed us. He stuck the handle of the scythe into the earth and let it go as he dropped to his knees, vanishing but for a gleam amongst the chest high stalks. The scythe bent over him like some curious long-necked, silver beaked bird, and as Grandad sobbed the wire jangled and twinged like tinny bells.

He grabbed handfuls of the cut wheat, its heads turned to dust under the pressure of his hands. He just sat there, suddenly still, the dust running through his clenched fingers and the sun gleaming on his armour of wire and ablaze in the blue of his mirrored sunglasses.

Margaret, tears wet on her face, suddenly ran forward. All blubbering she prised open his hands, taking the bundles of straw from his fist and pressed Zebediah into them.

"Don't be sad because you had to shoot all the animals, Grandad," she said. And with her little hands she bent the thin sheafs of stalk around each other, so they looked a rough straw doll of a beast. "We can make more, like you made Zebediah, and they'll be even more pretty and their spirits will wander the fields of heaven with Zebediah."

Grandad's head sprang up all of a sudden, like he'd heard a shot. He stood, all ajangle and glowing silver in the risen sun, and said, "These fields forgotten. This earth has forsaken us, but that is the way of earthen things. I love you kids. Let's forget this earth and have a celebration." He put his silver twined arm around Margie, smiling as they emerged from the wheat, and we walked back to the house.

"Steven," said Grandad as we finished wolfing the now cold breakfast, our stomachs rapacious with expectancy, "your father's black suit, the one he wore to Grandmother's, bless her soul, funeral, in the brown trunk, I think. Margaret, wear your mother's satin party dress. We'll rustle the best damn herd anyone's ever seen, and watch those duffers from the bank's faces when they come to auction off the beasts."

So I dressed in my father's black suit, which smelled of camphor, and Grandad found, rummaging in a box, Great Grandad's harness-racing silks, so over the top I wore a harlequin vest. Then Grandad tied a green and blue polka dot tie round the neck of my red shirt, and pinned his father's war medals on my chest.

Margie strolled out, beaming, in Mum's emerald satin party dress, too loose around her thin shoulders. So she tightened it up with sashes of silk around the waist, and a gold clasp that bunched up the baggy bosom, and draped herself in Mum's and her own jewellery so she glittered with chains of gold and brooches and pearls and rings, loose on her fingers.

Grandad strung his wires with the ring pulls off beer cans and brass washers and Christmas tree ornaments and bells, fridge magnets the shape of fruits and Disney characters and smiley faces, ribbons of aluminium foil and my old toy matchbox cars and keys and other bright metallic and jangling odds and ends, and stuck our Christmas Star in his cap.

Margaret put on her straw hat, and I donned my wide brimmed Akubra. Grandad pulled the brim so the hat sat at a jaunty angle and said, "Now. We're ready." He took his camera and set the timer so it trapped a photo of us together on the end of the porch, with the scattered bodies of chickens and Petersen leaping about behind us.

Then we pulled on our gumboots and Margaret said, "We look positively livid!" And I had to agree, dressed for the maddest Halloween costume party ever.

Then Grandad, with a jangle and a magician's flourish held up the tractor keys and said, in a solemn tone, "Mow the wheat field, Steven, my boy. Mow it all." He hadn't ever let me drive the tractor by myself, alone before, though I'd driven it a few times when he'd been out in Windorah.

I grabbed the keys and ran for the barn, waving my hat in the air and hollerin'.

"I want a good sized stack, ya hear?" he shouted then laughed.

Revelling in some mad and wanton power, I climbed into the cabin, adjusted the seat downwards and forwards, put in the key and pressed the starter. The engine kicked and I revved John Bell's 360 horses of Chevrolet engine so it shouted spumes of exhaust. I snapped on the stereo to a rock station, raised the harvester blades and roared out to the field.

I raised a hell of wheat dust and earth dust. Billows of ochre red chaff and the heavier dust of the earth, as I carelessly churned the ugly wheat. The dust raised and drifted for kilometres and turned the sky to a red rage, the sun within bloated and crimson. Under which I drove, so that this haze was a cloud of hate shrouding me, swirling against the cab windows, fingers of it, tendrils, battering and dissolving against the glass, as the tractor roared and I bellowed and the music blared. Inscribing a hexagrammatic mandala of my bitterness, my anger, upon that earth, no longer mine, that I had loved.

Then the habit of task superseded anger, bitterness, my savage joy and even my past love of that land, and I finished mowing the field with a care and an exactitude, writing an aeon old calligraphy rather than a scrawl. When the field was reduced to stubble, carpeted in straw, I lowered the hay grader on the back of Joh Bell and reversed, inscribing a star from points to centre, pushing the wheat into one enormous stack. The scythe, I realised, forgotten in my initial storm, my later calm, like the proverbial needle, lost in its depths.

Then I mowed the now wild straggle that edged the field, of Paterson's Curse, and pushed the tangle of it to the haystack. Mum had planted it when she'd kept an apiary, and I remembered the distinctive taste of the honey from those purple flowers, matured in big earthenware jars cool in the bottom shelf of the pantry, and how as a child in that treasure trove, Mum had caught me, my fingers sticky, sucking the sweetness from them. But all she said was how the scrubby, purple flowered weed was also called Salvation Jane. Then she dipped her fingers in the jar too.

When the sun was middling in the sky and the dust clouds had mostly settled, Grandad and Margaret drove out in the Ford pick-up, a tangled jigsaw of wire jangle-ing, teetering and towering in its tray.

Grandad waved a gleaming arm and I cut the tractor engine.

"Come on, Steven!"

"What do you think, Grandad?" I said with a nod towards the mountain of hay, edged with Paterson's purple tangles, that rose like some monstrous dusty bloom, as high as the house over the stubbled field.

"A veritable Himalaya, Steven my boy. An Ulluru of straw! The biggest mountain of hay in the world."

"It's ab-so-lute-ly livid!" said Margaret.

Grandad was excited. He was crazy excited. "We'll unload the pick-up and then have our picnic lunch."

He let down the tail gate and rolled a tar drum off the back of the Ford. Then we lashed some rope amongst the tangle of wire. We pulled at it, straining, and it rolled off, with a flutter of petals, like some enormous tumble weed, dropped a few curious wire shapes, and came to rest by the hay mountain.

The bottom of the pick up's tray was deep in flowers; irises and violets, chrysanthemums and marigolds, angel's trumpets and sprays and posies of seemingly, every last flower from Margaret's carefully tended garden.

We shovelled them off and the perfume crushed out of them, and they sat, a small brightly coloured hillock by the hay.

Margaret had spread a sumptuous lunch from a larder basket; of pickles and cold roast chicken, pizza slices and walnut cake and whipped cream, and plastic containers of syrupy peaches, and sticks of celery and cocktail onions, and mayonnaise and bread rolls, salads and mangoes and bananas and crystallised ginger, and tasty biscuits and tasty biscuits, and green and black olives and cubes of assorted cheeses, upon a lurid quilt of patchwork paisley.

While we feasted Grandad spoke of the city. Of dynamic ribbons and globe symbols, and banks and corporations and the *novus ordo seclorum*, of the over-organism, entitious without consciousness, of a generic symbology whose enticing heraldries were the blooms of corruption. Of continuous logos and static logoses. Of white noise and chaos. Of bleakness dressed in rainbows. Of how the city was a palace of mirrors, how the reversals of mirrors are lies, how, at least broken mirrors, shards, admit they lie. Of how many people are mirrors, are shards that do not know they are fragmentary, of contemporary man, convoluted of romanticism and cynicism. Of glass houses full of stone throwers.

And the sun bloomed on him, and silver light swelled from his face, incandescent. And we knew he was mad, but both Margie and I listened in rapture, to this man of wire and leather whose raucous laughter shook his body and rang the midday with jangling and tinkling and twangs and chimes. A discordant, but for that, a more delightful music.

"And now to work!" And we stood, brushing the crumbs from our finery.

Grandad and I started untangling shapes from the tumble of wire, while Margie packed away the luncheon. We stood the wire skeleta of cattle all around, and they cast thin, squiggly lined shadows on the dusty and stubbly earth.

Grandad with a long handled brush began ladling tar over the frames, and when he'd finished one Margie and I stuck sheafs of the hay, tangled with Paterson's Curse, to the legs, torsos and heads of the beasts, so that they were spindly legged and barrel chested.

Then, when a few were done and Grandad kept tarring and I kept tying on the hay, Margaret stuck a red Chrysanthemum to the end of each muzzle as a mouth, and violets or daisies or irises as eyes, and tied stiff straw tails to their rears. While she waited for me to finish she'd mottle the straw bodies with other flowers.

We worked, only stopping to drink Cokes or nibble at some cheese and biscuits from the basket. By three in the afternoon, when the sun was at its hottest and highest, and the blue as paling under that fire to a harshity of white, a magnificent herd of fat straw beasts stood quiet on the sun blasted pasture. We were tufted with straw and patched with petals and spattered with tar, and looked, as we stood admiring our beasts, like a trio of motley scarecrows.

Dog weary but happy we drove back to the house and cleaned up. We ate, then stood out on the porch and watched our herd, silhouetted, fat and proud, on the beckoning dusk.

My dreams that night were unremembered - but of soaring above and away, towards, then emerging from an unremitting turbulence.

The day opened with a raw crystalline light. In that shadowless predawn I ran out, for what I knew with the certitude of childhood's end would be the final time, to my tower. The structure seemed to rise up against the boiling blue of morning, a monochrome that in its oneness demanded hold of the infinite.

The grit of the rusting iron, as I climbed to that giddying height, into that blue void, was the stuff of the firmament.

So I remembered, the rust in my hands, it also towered after the long descent of evening, the world shrinking away below. But this turning was the tower's decline, and the curved horizon ever rising.

Over which, as I topped the platform and swung my back to the imminent sun, my arm hooked around the rust encrusted axle of the fan, against the screaming blue and a fat and livid daylight moon lowering on the horizon, blazed our golden and bejewelled herd.

As the sun then razed the dawn to day, blazed at my back and I felt its touches on the back of my neck and on my arms, and the shadow of the tower began its slow creep out, the tower declining all the while. And the farm under the first glow of that mocking liquid light, the miraculous beasts spread below, seemed a memento, a bizarre Calvary preserved under a dome of blue glass. For Grandad had taken his silver wire wrappings, my father's black suit, and mother's emerald dress, our fine costumes of yesterday complete with regalia, and made three

scarecrows, Curious shepherds overseeing the herd
from the height of wooden crosses.

Fleshed in straw and thistle and Paterson's Curse
Crimson mouthed and violet eyed
When the farm died
After the scorching months
We shot the herd
Took a thousand miles of baling wire
A thousand miles of rust flaked baling wire
and tied a hundred head of cattle
and three fine horse
and three fancy farmers
They stood proud, our golden calves
Then the rains blew in
And scattered them
And they rotted in the sun

Shake a Nativity under glass and snow falls. A
wind smelling fat with rain of a sudden shook this
earth, and the beasts bristled against it. The dust
raised and swirled, momentarily filling without
obscuring the dome of sky.

But the sun hauled down the earth, and the
shadow of my tower grew long, and it declined so
that I almost stood upon the ground. So too
lengthened the shadows of our quivering beasts, and
they seemed to move in fear. Golden calves before
some coming wrath.

A storm as black and immense as the onslaught of a winter's night swept over the horizon. The wind that gusted before it turned the blades of the mill, so they creaked around, rhythmically vibrating. The rust bitten vanes at the back snapped side to side in the gusts, like the tail of some ominous bird. And the earth tilted away and my tower seemed to rise and fly, as it flew I rode on the back of this malevolent bird, so fast towards the rushing blackness.

I clambered down and ran back to the house.

The rains, slow at first so the heavy drops kicked up spurts of dust, then of a sudden hammering, then slashing down, scattered our beasts. Tumbled them, stampeded them. Knocked them to earth, ate away their flesh of straw, plucked out their eyes and mouths and the brighter mottle of their hides, which floated away, a scum of petals on the flooding rivulets.

It thundered and flashed for only half an hour, We watched from the porch, distraught, this hell lit in lightening flashes. Then the sun came out, smeared over the slick earth. Quickly drying, glinting on the bent and tangled skeleta of our strewn beasts. Muddy clumps of straw began to ripen and rot, smelling like foul silage.

Grandad seemed transformed to his usual taciturn self, but we knew he wasn't; he was hurting as if cursed.

We took our cases and odds and ends and put them in the pick up. Margie clutched Zebediah in her hands. Grandad had an old and browning family photo in his lap.

The last I saw of the farm as we drove off for Windorah was a few lonely, bedraggled beasts of tattered straw and Paterson's Curse, the scythe, glinting, which somehow had remained planted in the earth, and we three fanciful scarecrows beside it.

Our flowered eyes weeping, our flowered mouths laughing.

A year or so later, in a southern suburb of Brisbane, in an ordinary life in which we walked to school rather than studying by relay satellite, Margaret wrote a poem that won a school competition, and was published in a local paper.

People asked me about the poem. Teachers, a journalist, Aunt May. What did Margaret mean by it?

So I wrote this story.

"She had a kind of grace, even as a small child, and also a kind of anguish. She brought herself here and threw herself down. In her letter she said there was a beauty here, and an incongruity. I see that."

Down in the arroyo, in the pit of the canyon, amongst the tumbled scree and bracken, the ironwork made a lattice of the sky, dizzying in its precise geometry. Small in the expanse of sand and wind carved rock, arid and alien in its hostility, Randall could also see that. The bridge in its order, the white van and the black SUV, the two men, one somber and stick thin in dark glasses and a crisp black suit, the other uncomfortable in a white plastic construction helmet, loose hi-vis vest over a technician's uniform of pale shirt and tan slacks, in that landscape wearied by aeons, a forgotten sea where only small thorned things clung to desperate lives, in that storm still and perilous beauty, men and their machines and constructions and platitudes were out of place.

"It's almost a year since she fell, since she threw herself down," said the gaunt man. The flowers in his hands, roses, lavender, in black cellophane, he threw down. They lay bright and forlorn against the rust red rocks, the sand moving in the wind, slowly consuming them. Not knowing now what to do with his hands, he crossed his arms, and held them tight against his ribs.

"They say because of who I was, other children treated her like a freak, that she was in love with death, because of my lyrics, because of my songs. You can lay it at the hands of the savagery of youth, or at these hands, that didn't protect her from that cruelty, but the truth is, some children have a grace that defies this world and its untold injuries, and so they fly."

"You're right, some children are too good for this world. I remember I thought that when it happened. When I saw it in the papers," said the technician. "Musician, aren't you?"

"I used to be. Sean Speck and The Last Days. I don't do that anymore. Now I'm just Sean Spencer."

"More of a Glen Campbell fan myself, than that rock music. Randall Candleman, safety engineer — they call me the bridge doctor." Candleman felt a brief urge to offer hands, but he held the transducer — a portable metal fatigue testing device like an electronic tablet with a cable and wand attached — tight in both hands, and his levity struck an off note, so as acknowledgment, a nod sufficed.

For a while, between them, there was nothing but the silence of slowly drifting sand, a silence Candleman broke, tapping the rusted rail twice with a knuckle. A faint ring answered across the span.

"The people that once lived here, in those caves up there, would say her voice is still on the wind."

"Because she killed herself?"

"Because she was never taken up. The first bridge here was built by an obscure branch of the

Puebloan people that lived in the cliff caves a thousand years ago. Not strictly a bridge, no. A spider spindle thing of hemp and wood and twisted vines still green with fruit and flowers, tethered to the trees either side of the canyon. Not a bridge between here and there," he said, pointing with the wand, "but a sky bridge for their burials. They would take the bodies of their dead out there, tied in something like a loose cocoon, suspended in the blue, and gather and sing a deep thrumming song that brought the hawks and the vultures. They would tear apart the dead, carrying the pieces into the sky. If the song was weak, if there was a storm, and the birds didn't come, if the body and the bridge just rotted and fell into the canyon, to be eaten by lizards and wolves, they would say her spirit couldn't find its way to the other world, that her voice was still on the wind."

Speck felt a tightening in his chest, he could hear an echo on the wind, a soughing, a childish voice lilting a verse about a mockingbird, a memory. "You're talking about my daughter," he said, his throat grinding.

"Sorry, sorry. I only meant, not her, but a thousand years ago," he said. "I read it in a book."

Candleman's voice trailed to a silence that left only the wind, a ringing like blood in Speck's ears. He tried to dismiss the noise. He wasn't sure what held him there. He turned to leave.

"I thought, at the time, I thought maybe she didn't kill herself," said Candleman. "This bridge is notorious you know. Dangerous."

"What exactly do you mean by that?" Speck was thinking of the gun under the car seat, consumed by red rage. The stuttering image of him pulling the slide, jamming at against Candleman's temple. He could leave this fool here for the sand and the scorpions to eat. Or himself. But no, he'd got rid of the gun months ago.

"The bridge is a killer. No listen. I don't just test the metal. I study the places I have to check. In the midst of the great storm of 1849 the cavalry wiped out the natives that lived here, so the railway company could build this bridge. The natives pulled in their ladders and rope bridges, but they didn't resist, most of them didn't even hide. They sang. The bodies fell from the caves and the cliff tops. Those that stayed in the back of the caves, the old, the infirm, the children, the soldiers dashed their brains out with rifle butts, or just pitched them over the edge. Flood waters rushed down the canyon, down the arroyo, scattering the dead across the desert plain. In their mythology, they didn't go up, but went down, to some kind of cold and miserable underworld. A few, the soldiers left alive. A few girl children." Speck was clenching and unclenching his fists. He had long, powerful looking fingers, big hands and bony wrists jutting from his sleeves. Frankenstein's monster's hands, Candleman thought. He wondered if Speck had those strangler's hands because he was a musician, or if he was musician because he had those hands?

"In 1853 they finished the bridge. It was meant to open up gold fields in the Southern Sangre De Cristo Range, but the gold there played out after only a few years. The first official train across, which joined this spur line from Santa Fe, taking dignitaries, miners and their families, well, they say she bent sideways, threw off a locomotive and train of four passenger cars, coal car, mail car, the whole kit and caboose, into the arroyo, here below, then raised herself up so as except for a splintered railing, you wouldn't even know she buckled."

"The theory is, it was a kind of oscillation, set up by the rhythm of the train, that ran through the bridge like a wave. 'A fearful symmetry', an engineer at the time called it. Eighty-seven souls lost. They added these cross braces and extra supports. It never happened again, but there were collisions, derailments. Falls. Of course it's a walking bridge now, part of the national park, it hasn't carried a train in 150 years. They say a tourist fell to his death just a few months ago, struck by an eagle. He climbed the safety rail and had his ear pressed to the old iron. They added a higher rail last year. I couldn't tell you the number of…" Candleman had somehow circled around to the subject he had been trying to avoid.

"Suicides," Speck finished. "Isabel moved down here, to Cross Canyon, the town near the edge of the park, to do an internship as a ranger – a conservation officer. She loved it here. She left a note. Not explicit, but not ambiguous either."

"I couldn't imagine. I'm so sorry," said Candleman. This time, he seemed to understand, that for such loss, the condolences of strangers were superfluous, like a language you once understood, but had forgot.

"Why did he climb the rail?"

"There's a story. They say the old iron remembers. There is a sound in the metal. A song, a thrum, a heartbeat. If you place your hand against it, if you listen carefully, when the wind is rushing down the canyon, you can feel the temperature change, you can hear the voices of the lost, same say you can hear the life taken up by the bridge, pulsing."

"Who says? Who are these 'they' you keep talking about?"

"You know. The old-timers, the locals, the grapevine, eyewitnesses, reports."

"They say eyewitnesses are unreliable, the worst kind of evidence," countered Speck.

"Hey, they don't call me The Bridge Doctor for nothing." Candleman pulled something like a gleaming metal octopus with one great eye from his pocket. A stethoscope. "We can listen for ourselves."

Speck could again, almost make out the words, a lilting, childish sing-song on the wind…Daddy's gon' a buy you a mockingbird…a fading memory.

Speck took the stethoscope. "Do you use that in your work?"

"No," said Candleman. "Not really. The guys at county gave it to me as a kind of joke. Though I don't just check bridges. Any critical steel framed structure. Buildings, storage tanks, refineries, transmission towers, radio telescopes, satellite dishes. The thing is, I've used it. I've listened to each building, each frame, each tower, each bridge, and they all have a different sound."

"How do they sound?"

"Oddly enough, you can kind of hear a wail in them, a low miserable wail, when the metal is sick. I've confirmed it with the transducer. I checked the Apache Canyon Railroad Bridge, that's a deck plate girder bridge in Santa Fe County, built in 1894, and it sings a pure sweet note, like running your finger on the edge of a wine glass. I once listened to the Upper Canyon Diablo trestle, the original, not the replacement, up in AZ, it screamed like breaking glass. When I tested both of those with the transducer – it uses ultrasonic and subsonic waves to check for metal fatigue, crystalline fractures, rust, density flaws, and all the other weaknesses metals are prone to, the Apache Canyon was fine, and the Diablo needed to be replaced."

"And this one? Does this bridge have a name? Have you listened to this bridge? What bloody song does it sing?"

"Oh, this one has no name I know of. A map reference, maybe a code number in the annals of the Atchison, Topeka, and Santa Fe Railroad, but no name, and it's my first time here. I haven't heard it sing."

"Give me those." Speck took the stethoscope, placed the tubes in his ears. He walked over to the pylon. He had to pull himself up a little against the footing, the rough old concrete stained yellow by desert sands, the embedded pebbles, showing through, polished and black like eyes.

The bridge hung over him. He reached up and placed the mouth of the thing against the metal. He heard its heartbeat, as Candleman had said. Something like the pounding rhythm of a train, coming closer. Then a sound like fire. Then perhaps a choir, distant, something low and mournful. Then the lilting, child's song…if that mockingbird don't sing… London Bridge is falling down, falling down…my fair lady…

The whisper faded. It was somehow like the voice was still there, but he was becoming deaf to it, he was falling away. "I can't hear it anymore. I heard her singing, but I can't hear her anymore."

"Listen, wait. I'll send a wave through it, a pulse, with the transducer, both nodes. What can you hear? That will make it vibrate." Candleman reached up and placed the tip of the wand against the girder.

A wrenching scream, a metal keening threw Speck to his back on the sand.

"What was that? I heard that? What was that?" Candleman was shouting. His face looked clown-pale, mouthing speech. His words were thick like he was under water. Speck could still hear the scream, like metal wheels, like falling.

Something hit Candleman in the chest with a whomp. He fell back and sprawled. The transducer tangled in his hand as he tried to gain purchase to get up. With a high sheik something else hit him. Talons ripped his cheek. A bird, something like small brown-speckled hawk was scrabbling at his face, trying to get at his eyes under the hard hat.

Above, past the ironwork lattice, above the arches, in the desert blue, a cloud swirled and thickened, something like smoke, something like a tornado. Speck pulled himself to his feet and ran, arms raised, shouting at Candleman to run, to the van. Small birds beat at his neck with fierce wings, scratching with needle claws, tearing pieces from his ears, flying up with gobbets in their beaks. His sleeves were shredded, blood pouring from his wrists. The door handle slippery in his grasp.

Candleman was almost to his van when out of the swirl an eagle struck, not a bald eagle, but something angular and dark, blood blossomed in long rents on his back as the weight of the creature smashed him into the door. It swirled away, wings beating, blood dripping from meat in its claws. Candleman scrambled into the van as the cloud for a moment obscured the van.

There seemed to be an order in the madness of the birds. They swirled in the cloud, the bright and the dark, the fierce and the plain, the raptor and the prey, until by some ill reason one stooped from the mass, swooping out of the sky to rake and peck and shriek and batter with frenzied wings.

Speck hit the side of the SUV like a tackle. He jammed the handle up and down. Locked! He could see the keys in the ignition. A silver blur struck his shoulder, ripping through fabric, into the flesh. It jabbed at his face, striking for the eye with a hooked yellow-tipped beak, hitting so hard the lens of his sunglasses starred. He batted it away with a forearm, dragging at the rear door handle. Wrenching it open on hands and knees he clambered in. As he sat up there was a buzzing, an insectoid whirr. A tiny bird, jewelled wings a blur hung in the air in front of his face, lapping at the blood that pooled at the rim of his glasses and dripped down his cheek with a long tongue. It watched him with red fixed glare, seemingly mesmerised. Ruby drops dripped on its emerald chest. He slammed it into the window glass, held it there scratching at his fingers until he could hit the switch in the armrest to lower the window. He palmed it out the gap, and it vanished back into the wing storm. He reversed the switch and the window edged back into place, and he struggled into the front seat.

The cloud swirled, and another bird swooped out of the swarm, this time something small and grey and swift. It battered at the windscreen then swept off again. For the life of him Speck couldn't help but think of one of those peculiar 19th century dances, where enlivened by music and the cheers participants would take turns coming out of the crowd and performing a strut, part walk, part dance down an aisle comprised of their fellows. The thought of it unleashed something from inside his chest, a shriek, a howl of laughter.

As if in response, the *ussussurus* of wing beats faded. He could see the cloud of a sudden disperse like thrown ashes. There was a metal keening on the wind that rose and rose until it was like a scream in his ear and he grasped his head in both hands.

High above a ripple ran through the bridge. With an earthquake roar the entire structure seemed to buckle sideways, pulling from the face of the rock and tipping, then in front of Candleman's van two great pylons lifted from the floor of the canyon, in a haze of dust and crumbling cement, then those great feet stepped sideways and planted themselves more firmly in the earth, and the bridge poised for a moment, like a coursing beast testing the air. Then in one lumberous and shrieking moment it stepped again, curving its back and its entire length, and bent one end down, as if to take a close and ravenous look at the small thing on the ground between its feet.

Then, with a hungering and deliberate purpose, it stepped forward.

Candleman was gesticulating wildly from the cab of his van, mouthing something, when the great concrete sheathed pylon came down and crushed it like a tin can under a booted heel.

Speck turned the ignition and drove, out along the arroyo, toward where a trail wound up the hill into the south west edge of the national park.

Through the dust cloud in the rear view mirror, he could see the bridge, the concrete crumbling away from its girder pylon limbs as with a piston motion, part animal, part machine, it dismembering Candleman's van. As he lost view it was batting at the wreckage like a cat with broken mouse.

He thought, I'm hallucinating. But he wasn't hallucinating. He thought, this is hell —nor am I out of it. He thought of home, the ranch on the outskirts of Santa Fe. At the top as he swung onto the road through the park, making for the highway, the tips of the Sangre de Cristo range red in the setting sun, the hunched and silent shoulders of the mountains now in shadow, he saw the thing in the distance, cresting the hill, a silhouette against the violet sky. It swayed back and forth, searching. Then it came.

He could only think of one thing, if this thing was going to destroy him, he would see Isabel one more time, or at least, be at her grave. At the highway he turned south toward Gila and Cross Canyon, the town where she had lived, where under ugly red sandstone, she was buried.

Speck drove, fast, the car shuddering. The radio blared one of his own songs, these are days of dogs and metal...he was shrieking. The metal thing, he could now only barely conceive of it as a bridge, was loping in the distance, some vast sextipedal beast. The birds still swirled around it the way small scavenger fish follow a shark, waiting for carrion and carnage.

Against the horizon in its fire, the monster ran, pacing, taking obstacles black in the twilight with the grace of a loping hound, with indefatigable purpose, a machine-like insectoid articulation. Like the song, above the engine roar and the drone of tyres, a metal scream sawed at his ears with a ragged breath-like rhythm.

For a moment on the dark sides of the mountain he lost sight of it, then it seemed to be far away, on the edge of the sierra, four arched legs fixed to the mountainside, bent upwards, the two forward pylons clawing at the brightening constellations, standing rampant, its jutting cantilever platform raised up and roaring silently into the night.

He could see the sleepy yellow lights of the town, winking on in the dusk. The graveyard ahead, just a turn off the highway through a rose tangled white picket trellis, held orderly rows of simple markers in marble and sandstone, freshly mown lawns, benches under lamps. It was even called a park, Cross Canyon Park, as if its visitors could pack up their frisbees and baskets and Gingham blankets at the end of the day and depart.

From the gate he could see her stone, even in the oncoming dark. Though not ostentatious, a plain block of orange and tan marbled sandstone, with her named, and her dates, and the inscription, Ever Loved, it was large, a supine megalith, overshadowing the more ornate and traditional markers around it. He thought now he was free of the thing, now it had disappeared into the wilderness, he would call someone. They would lock him up, but they could go and see where the bridge had been, themselves. They could follow the trail it tore through the earth. First he needed to see Isabel. He needed her forgiveness, simply for all those absences. He thought, after all, that's what it was.

Then with a squeal the bridge reared up on the black and stone jagged horizon, crushing fences, breaking and scattering markers, its girder legs piercing deep into the soft earth, so plumes of it erupted as it stepped.

The birds that rode its girders and railings, flew from that uncertain perch and settled in rows on every cross and arch and on the wide stone arms and wings of angels.

The bridge stalked forward, like a centaur, or a vulture, then stopped and shook itself so more birds scattered, in a fury of caws and metal. It raised its forelimbs high with an awkward piston savagery bringing them down so her stone cracked in pieces. It hung above her grave with blunt limbs tearing and ripping jackhammer blows at the earth.

Speck's chest swelled with agony. He gulped air into his lungs, tasting damp earth and ozone and hot iron, something alien and avian, and something like mouldering leaves, only ranker. His neck pulsed, his throat tightened like the skin of a drum, and he let out a long fierce wail that tore at his chest, and rang in his throat like it was brass, one high resonant note of anguish, and a deeper one that ached his ribs that joined it.

aaaaaaaaaaaaaaaaaaaaaaaaaaaaaaaaaaaaaaaaaaaaaaaaaa aaaaaaaaaaaaaaaaaaaaaaaaaaaaaaaaa
      aaaaaaaaaaahhhhhhhhhhhhhhhhhhhhhhhhhhhhhhhhhhhhh hhhhhhhh

A lament that stilled the trees and silenced the wind. The sound of breaking, the shriek of metal in his ears stopped. He could hear a fading ticking, the resigned creak of cooling iron, as the bridge, like some weary pet, lay down across the grass and gravestones and slept.

There amongst the torn and quiet girders she stood, pale and aglow, finger to her black lips, until the darting shadows of the birds tore the shade apart and fled, carrying her up.

When the last white wisp of her was gone, when all the birds had flown, when all that remained was the torn earth, the broken stones, the still and rusting iron, Speck turned away. He got in the car and drove.

He thought it was a dream. That he was still in it. He could still see it laying there in his rear view, as on the other side of town he swept up the curve of the interstate onramp.

There was a metal keening on the wind. He saw the sign for the Cross Canyon-Santa Fe Highway Bridge. A bridge over endless black ribbons, going nowhere. He felt in his bones, through his hands tightening on the wheel, through the metal of the car, through the whirr of the tyres, in the steel and concrete, a deep and resonant hum.

About the Author

C S Hughes grew up by the bellow and stink of cattle yards, and the hollow and roar of dunes. He says he was a hobo in his youth, and later worked as a spice seller, a book dealer, and a trader in junk and assorted detritus.

More recently he has been a writer and editor of poetry books, editing *From The Ashes – Poetry In Support Of Bushfire Relief, The Poetry Of John Ashdown-Hill* and *Somnia Blue,* amongst others.

He has been published online and in print in *Blue Pepper, Five 2 One, Weird Tales, Sampietrino, The Blue Nib* and various others. He has published several collections of his own work, including, *The Little Book Of Funerals, The Book Of Whimsies, Sound Never Dies & Other Poems,* the short story collection *The Book Of Fables,* and the novella in verse, *COVID-22.*

He currently lives in the Gippsland Lakes region of Victoria with a cat and an historian, where he (still) studies and dabbles in photography, poetry and story writing, but claims, with a nearly straight face, to mostly being a hobo.

www.ingramcontent.com/pod-product-compliance
Lightning Source LLC
Chambersburg PA
CBHW021117130626
46554CB00002B/743